A HISTORY OF
HEARTACHE

A HISTORY OF HEARTACHE

Patrick Strickland

STORIES

MELVILLE HOUSE
BROOKLYN • LONDON

A History of Heartache : Patrick Strickland

First published in 2026 by Melville House

First Melville House Printing: January 2026

Distributed by Penguin Random House LLC,
1745 Broadway, New York, NY 10019
www.penguinrandomhouse.com

The following stories have previously been published: "A History of Heartache" in *The Coachella Review*; "Mockingbird" in *The Broadkill Review*; "Magic" in *Cowboy Jamboree*; "Rent Money" in *Pithead Chapel*; "Screaming East on I-10" in *Cleaver*; "Dead Cats" in *South 85 Journal*; "General Holy War" in *Porter House Review*; "Sometime in Late '87, Early '88" in *Five South*; "That Fire's the Whole World" in *Peatsmoke Journal*; "2008" in *Flash Fiction* Magazine; "Rooster" in *New World Writing Quarterly*; "Ice Man" in *The Barcelona Review*; "The Han Gil Hotel" in *Epiphany: A Literary Journal.*

Melville House Publishing
46 John Street
Brooklyn, NY 11201

and

Melville House UK
Suite 2000
16/18 Woodford Road
London E7 0HA

mhpbooks.com
@melvillehouse

ISBN: 978-1-68589-235-7
ISBN: 978-1-68589-236-4 (eBook)

Designed by Beste M. Doğan

Printed in the United States of America
1st Printing
A catalog record for this book is available from the Library of Congress

The authorized representative in the EU for product safety and compliance is Easy Access System Europe, Mustamäe tee 50, 10621 Tallinn, Estonia.
gpsr.requests@easproject.com

For Ann

As for the emotional concentration of
our anger . . . it is a matter of indifference what its
sources are—even if it is a rage which derives
from drugs, we must be able to incorporate it.
—William Herrick, *Love and Terror*

A HISTORY OF HEARTACHE

A HISTORY OF HEARTACHE

When Ma starts in on me again, she's splashing gas station cabernet into an old, cracked coffee mug, flipping the bottle top-down and filling it to the lip. The springs from the pullout couch dig into my ass, and I can't get comfortable. Ma grabs the remote and hits mute. A guy on TV sobs silently, his head in his hands. He lost someone he loves, I guess, but who hasn't?

I listen to noise claw all about the trailer—dishwasher whooshing, dryer thumping, strays scraping at the back door. Nothing's out of the ordinary, not really, but it's one of those nights when you feel like someone snuck in and adjusted all your furniture just a couple centimeters.

"If you don't want to be here, I don't want you here," Ma says. She doesn't mean it. She just gets all pushy after her third glass, starts mouthing off with stuff she doesn't mean. Inside, she's feeling lonesome. I know this because she's been playing Roy Orbison all night back in her bedroom, the same tired, old tunes she listened to when my old man ran out on us.

Three months stand between me and graduation. I'm already plotting to take to the open highway, imagining my pickup topping a hundred and blasting past billboards advertising hot showers and truck stop kolaches. My buddy John keeps saying we ought to ditch town together. He won't stop going on about New York because he thinks no one there has ever heard of this town. I'm not so sure. I have my eyes set on California. I've seen the photos, big, blue waves surging up like mountains and hitting the shore, and can practically feel the cold water numbing my bones.

"I don't know, Ma," I tell her.

"You think you and Suzie can make it work, huh? When your dad went off to school, you think I didn't know he was dirty dickin' other girls?" Ma asks. She won't just come out and say it, that she doesn't have anyone left but me.

"I don't even know if we'll stay together," I say. Ma cocks an eyebrow. I throw my hands up.

She downs half her glass in one swig and refills. She tends bar at the VFW and knows better. She has a history of heartache, most of which she drums up all on her own nowadays.

I stand up, pace around the living room for a minute. Plastic wrappers and empty Hungry-Man boxes cover the coffee table. I chew the words slowly in my head before I speak. Anything can set her off crying nowadays. Sometimes she comes home from the bar in tears. Her customers all love her, she says, but they're a rough crowd. They grab her ass and holler all night. They hurl bottles at her if she takes her time with their Bud Lights.

The phone saves me. I snatch it from its cradle before the second ring. I haven't even said hello yet and John blurts out, "You ever see whatever's inside someone's head split wide open?" He loves to talk like this, a real tough guy.

"What?"

"Just pick me up. Bring those baseball bats. They still in the bed of your pickup?"

"Yeah," I say, slamming the phone down and stuffing my feet into my sneakers. I make for the front door.

"Where are you—" Ma says, but I'm gone before she can spit out the words.

I pull up and find John pacing around in his driveway. His family isn't well off, but he lives in a real house, one with a concrete foundation. He slides into the passenger seat and rubs his eyes until they're pink. He's sweating beer. I asked what happened, but it's the same as always. His dad laid into him again, something about sneaking Coors Light from the garage fridge. His old man is a real hard-ass, a marine.

John rifles around in my glove box and finds the pill stash I store there for emergencies. I cribbed them from Ma; she's got all types of anxiety meds, stuff that hits your head like a hammer. He hands me a tramadol and I swallow it dry. He can't keep anything at home because his mom searches everywhere: his backpack, underwear drawer, the air-conditioning vents. She's as bad as his old man, always trying to catch him in the deed. One time she splattered ketchup all over her white shirt and said she had been attacked while taking out the trash, all just to see if John was sloshed enough to believe her.

It doesn't matter where you are in this town; the glow from the football stadium burns the night sky purple. Must be nine, maybe ten o'clock, but I can never know for sure because my radio doesn't work. The pickup rattles like an earthquake over a pothole. It's an old truck, a '94 Ford I inherited from my big brother Hank, but I can't bring myself to replace it. I can't even move into his old room, the way Ma sits in there half the day fingering his photos and sniffing his shirts. Grief can be strange like that.

I floor it and slam through every red light between John's house and Barton Middle School. "I used to take these same ones," John says. He pops a pill in his mouth and starts chewing on it.

"Oh, yeah?" I say, but I've already heard it all. The guy gets sentimental every time he starts tipping them back. He's all sob stories tonight.

"If I had only juked right instead of left, he would've missed me altogether. My ACL would work fine. Worst moment of my life," he says. The real bitch of it is you just can't shut him up no matter how much time's passed. He means six seconds of a football scrimmage that happened in the eighth grade. A linebacker knocked him on his back and bent his leg crooked. He's convinced he's the first person who's ever had tough luck. It's not like I don't get it—why he roots around in his past for a better him—but poor John has gone wild for pills ever since.

Over in the passenger seat, he is still gnawing on the pill. It takes all I have not to stomp on his knee. "Can you not just swallow that fuckin' thing?" I snap.

In the parking lot outside Barton Middle School, John and I are treading in circles between the pools of lamppost light that puddle on the pavement. He says four or five boys from across the highway are on the way. Someone wants to scrap him. John stole the guy's girlfriend way back when, or the guy stole John's girlfriend the other day. It's hard to follow.

Somewhere nearby crickets click and click. I stop listening to John. Kids in town are always brawling in parking lots, always busting each other up with empty beer bottles or tiny garden shovels, and no single reason why is better than the next. I can't get into a good school, I think, but California has plenty of two-years.

John swings the bat over and over like he is nailing one over the back fence in left field. He throws his hands up and trots around all celebratory. Now he makes like he is bashing someone on the pavement. He beats the hell out of his own shadow. I prop mine, a Louisville Slugger I snagged from Hank's room, on my shoulder. It's not like he'll need it anymore.

Some big shot magazine reporter flew down from New York or Washington D.C. and took photos of Ma and me on the front porch. Kids were dying all over town. Hank was sixteen when we found him. The reporter took off his glasses and kept scribbling in a yellow legal pad and said, "But why did Hank choose to do heroin?"

"Choose?" Ma said. I put a soft hand on her shoulder, but she sputtered like a broken radio. "Choose? *Choose.*" The reporter drove off in his rental. I wondered how he made sense of us, if he'd ever met anyone like us before. The story was published a month later with the headline TEXAS HEROIN MASSACRE.

A lamppost burns out and all the shadows make Barton look like a prison. I turn to John and say, "You didn't go to school here, did you?"

"We went to Barton together," he tells me, all huffy and offended. He likes to play mean, but he's always getting hurt when I forget the history we share. I just like to fuck with him. He nods toward the school. "We literally went to school here together. You've known me since sixth grade, man."

"Yeah, that's good," I say. He looks at me like I killed his dog, and I did, but it was a long time ago, maybe a year or two now, an accident backing out of his driveway, drunk. "You know, Barton is a real shit school."

We are waiting in the parking lot. Everything feels sideways. All of a sudden, headlights stripe our chests. The first pickup growls its way into the parking lot. It's a muscular Dodge, sits high up on mudders. A Chevy crawls in behind it, a new one with an extended cab. There's a grill guard on its face. The tramadol I swallowed hits me. For a moment, the truck looks like an armored vehicle, the kind of thing John's old man rode around in over in Fallujah.

There's a crowd of boys crouched down in the truck beds. John heaves the baseball bat from his shoulder and it clunks on the bed of my pickup. A tall boy jumps down. He is blond and lean, smiles with what I admit are real nice teeth, but he stalks around like he thinks he's Mike Tyson. I remember his face from some place I cannot remember. His boots stamp on the pavement. He balls and un-balls his fists, over and over. "What y'all planning with those bats?"

I have no clue, but mine is still in my hands, and my hands are trembling.

Last Friday, I picked up my girlfriend, Suzie, from her place off 18th. We made a few laps around the eastside and parked down at Bob Woodruff Park, not far from the pond. She flicked a soft pack of Parliament Lights until one fell out in her hand. We sprawled out on the bed of my truck. The ducks wouldn't let up. We tried to tally the clouds but kept losing count. She laid her head on my chest, and I pulled her in close. "What're you thinking?" she said.

I asked her to make off to California with me. She sat up and pressed her palms hard on both my cheeks, stared at me. "You're batshit, aren't you?" she said.

I nodded. We eased onto our backs again, but the clouds had snarled together. There was no hope. "Well, why not?"

"Okay, well if you mean it, I will give it a think," she said, but she made her mind up before I drove her home.

"You have no job there," she said, and I told her, "I have no job here."

"We'll be real poor there," Suzie said. She's always doing this kind of thing, coming down on me like a sledgehammer.

I yanked my empty pockets inside out. "We aren't exactly rolling in it here. Besides, I thought you loved me."

"I never said that."

"It was implied."

"Not by me."

I came this way the other day. Ma and I went into the Walgreens across the street. She shoved a few wadded bills across the counter. "Sorry," she said to the pharmacist and damn near ran out of the place with a sackful of anxiety pills the doctor keeps her on.

Right now, a guy in a blue polo is locking the pharmacy up. I can see him as he pulls the metal shutters down in front of the sliding glass doors. He walks over to the 7-Eleven, its orange-and-green lights smoldering like a roadside casino.

"Four or five boys?" I ask John, but he just shrugs. Actually, there are fifteen, maybe twenty of them cracking their knuckles. "It's a goddamn cavalry."

The Louisville Slugger won't do me any good, so I toss it in the truck bed. The boys move our way. A few of them smile. A police cruiser speeds right by and never slows down.

I remember what Hank told me about boys from across the highway. He used to say those boys eat steak and potatoes every night and whoop our asses in football, but they have too many rules and fight without heart.

A junkie wails on the pay phone outside the 7-Eleven and falls on his knees, clutching his knuckles.

I make knots of my hands. I tense my body. Ma would flip if she knew where I am. I can already see her face, bent everywhere, puffy in places, and damp with tears. "You better stay put," I tell John, but he is already inching away. The boys from across the highway form half a circle around me. "John," I say, but it's no use.

The boys swarm me, and I land one good punch, maybe two, but they tumble down on top of me like something chucked from the sky. A boot bashes my skull, knuckles knock something loose in my eye socket, and a body crashes down on my back. I cough ragged into the pile.

When I look up through a tangle of arms and legs, the junkie across the street is rolling around on the ground, bawling. A 7-Eleven clerk snatches him by the shirt collar. The clerk tries to drag him to his feet, but the guy is all lead.

John is tearing ass right into the shadows of the scrimmage field next to the middle school. I wonder how he runs so fast with a bum knee.

The police cruiser circles back and slides into the parking lot. Its blue-and-red lights glaze the school walls. The pile lifts off me, the boys from across town scatter, and I dive behind a bush. My skull throbs like something is trying to break out of it. The cop can't find me, gives up, and swings a hard right on Park Avenue. The cruiser gets smaller the farther he goes. I almost step on a syringe and think of all the ailments I almost contracted.

I drive across the road and find John behind 7-Eleven.

The junkie waves our way, but I tell him to eat it. His face crumbles, a real sad sight. I feel bad immediately and wonder if he has a family somewhere, maybe a wife and kids all hungry and sad, but John jumps in and rolls down the window. I stomp on the gas and the pickup shrieks out of the parking lot. He lifts a fist, clenching his wadded-up boxers, and confesses he shit himself while some of the boys gave him chase.

Before we hit his street, he pitches the soiled briefs at someone's azaleas. "When did you even take those off?" I say.

"How could I explain that to my old man?" he says, half his forearm in my glove box, digging around for the pill bottle.

I feel a shiner welling up beneath my right eye. Blood is drying on my palms. I laugh, but I feel lonesome thinking of what to tell Ma when I appear in the drive all banged up. What will she say when I load up the pickup and leave for good?

I tell John, "I don't know."

I grip his shoulder, clamp down hard. "John, I do not know." I squeeze tighter and he winces. I could crush him, but he's been through enough already. "I have no idea, John. I do not know."

MOCKINGBIRDS

It's around five-thirty when I clock out. Mike is protesting outside the clinic again. He's got this handwritten placard that says something about a big baby-killing conspiracy. He thinks I'm the ringleader. Every time a car blasts past, he waves his arms all about. He starts screaming as soon as he spots me stepping outside. He does this three, maybe four times a week. I don't know how he does it, cares so much.

I started working at the East Side Family Planning Clinic five years ago, only a few months after the school district canned me. I just shine the shitter and mop the floors—that's my whole job. But you wouldn't know it from the way Mike talks about me. He's had it out for me ever since I slapped his phone from his hand while he filmed a young lady, just a girl really, leaving the clinic.

Every chance he gets, he films me and posts the video on his Facebook. When I leave work, he tails me, telling all his followers that I am the mastermind behind this big industrial-scale baby-killing operation. If you watched his videos, you'd think I rip the babies out with my bare hands. I have no clue what's happened in his life, what's gutted him so deeply that he needs to bust my balls, but you'd think I swing the babies around by their little limbs.

Dealing with Mike takes composure, so I pause in the doorway and wait a moment. A little sliver of air conditioning crawls up my back. I step into the humidity. Over on the corner, Mike stands tall on his toes. He goes by PatriotVeteran1492 online. Last year, I found his real name—Mike—on Google, and it riles him up. He's a real hothead, always throwing his arms up and screaming himself hoarse. "Mike," I sometimes yell, and it's like clockwork, the way he melts down and sputters everywhere, spitting all over the sidewalk.

I look back at the clinic. It isn't much, a big gray crate that could have been airlifted in from Russia or any other place with big gray crates for buildings. The windows are tinted black, and the sign says EAST SIDE FAMILY PLANNING. All that's to say, there's nothing special about the clinic. But the way Mike glares at it wildly, you'd think he unearthed a mass grave right here in town.

I hear the door open behind me and look back. It's the security guard, Ed. He's standing sideways in the doorway, staring past me. He's got his eyes fixed on Mike. His arms are crossed, his face all stern. "You want me to escort you to the car, Phil?" he says.

"No, Ed," I tell him. I'm tired, and my voice is all throat today. "I can handle it. Thanks, though."

My pickup is parked in the lot across the street. I have to pass Mike to get to it. I start making my way, but then I notice an image of my face printed on his T-shirt, all bunched up and wrinkled.

My wife is nearby. She died five years back, but I can feel her presence. "That's a terrible photo of you, Phil," she whispers in my ear. She used to be real sweet, but ever since she passed, all we do is argue. She flits around behind me and puts me down. A real piece of work. I tell her I love her. I try to remind her of how happy we were together. She won't hear any of it, but I keep at it, trying to win her back.

"Tammy, doll," I say. "You don't have to say stuff like that. I already know you're out of my league."

Mike smiles a big smile as I walk up. It's July, and the sun has done a real number on him. His face is all red. He's drenched in sweat. Right beneath my face, in big block letters, his shirt says: PHILLIP TURP KILLS BABIES

ALL DAY AND NIGHT. He's got my name spelled wrong, and there are so many words they hardly fit.

Summers burn cruel here. Nowadays Tammy calls me a sweaty pig, but she was singing a different tune when she was still alive. She used to say the heat taught us to appreciate the little morsels of relief. She meant a small breeze, a spurt of AC, a patch of shade under a sycamore. She said it just like that: *morsels.* She went wild for words like that. The first few months after she died, she didn't appear much. I used to whisper her words. Crying, I'd wander the aisles of Kroger's muttering *morsels, kernels.* At home on the couch, watching a ballgame on TV, I'd catch myself saying *itty bitties.*

I stop in front of Mike and palm a crumpled pack of Lucky Strikes. One falls out in my hand and I fire it up, my first smoke since lunch. I blow a lungful at Mike and smile through the clouds of smoke. He puffs his chest. I spent the whole day crawling up under the clinic beds to clean them, and my back throbs something terrible. Sunlight snaps off car mirrors and damn near blinds me. The ammonia soaked into my skin rolls my stomach. But Mike doesn't seem to notice any of it. He just keeps swinging his placard.

I take a closer look. It says, PHIL TURP: BABY EXECUTIONER.

Tammy was brought up south of Waco in Walnut Estates Trailer Community, a fifteen-unit lot crammed with double-wides, thick chickweeds, and trash mounds. We met in a buffet line at Luby's. She asked if I was planning on taking all the mashed potatoes for myself. We hit it off right away. She was twenty-one, four years younger than me, but we didn't care. She had just graduated from Waco Community College with a two-year degree, and I was a summer semester away from finishing a physical education degree that mowing lawns and taking out loans had paid for. We would stay up in bed all night, Tammy and me, waiting for the sun to reach through the blinds. We would plot plans to move far away and raise a crop of Little League all-stars. The doctor had told me a few years earlier that my swimmers were no good, but I never let on—those days I was still clinging onto a morsel of hope.

Her old man had served in Nam. After he married and had Tammy, he busted his ass in a garage seven days a week, banging a wrench on rusted-out motors, patching tires, all that. Her mom passed the days clipping coupons and screaming at the unemployment office on the phone.

An eighteen-wheeler had ripped off my mom's and

dad's heads when I was sixteen, and I was still wading in the grief that welled up inside me. I ran through a twelve-pack of Bud Ice a night, and sometimes I tossed in half a bottle of Wild Turkey. Once every couple weeks, I staggered home from the bar with gnarled knuckles and black eyes, my shirt slit to shreds. No matter what mess I made, Tammy and her parents treated me like family. You hear about that kind of love—you just don't imagine you'll ever find it.

We tied the knot in her backyard. It was a small ceremony. Her mom had strung up Christmas lights on the chain-link fence behind the trailer. Tammy and I swayed side to side, slow dancing, and then we all plopped down in lawn chairs. Her cousin Earl, who lived three trailers down, stood up in front of us. He wore a clip-on tie and delivered the toast with a can of Miller High Life. Fireflies lit up around us. Everyone cried, even me. Her mom and dad and cousin all slapped me on the shoulder and cracked big smiles. You'd have thought we were hauling off for Hollywood. Tammy's old man took me aside and clamped a coarse hand on my collarbone. "I know you'll do right by her," he said.

"Thank you," I told him, and I meant it because you don't forget a moment like that.

The next morning, Tammy and I loaded the few items we owned into my pickup: a big beer box full of Tammy's old romance paperbacks, a few garbage sacks stuffed with shirts and shoes, and an Igloo keeping cool a twelver of Bud Ice for the road. I splashed Wild Turkey into a Diet Coke can, cranked the engine, and we pushed north to Plano, our hearts full of a hope I had never known.

I had lined up a good gig at Armstrong Middle School, teaching physical ed to the handicapped kids and coaching the seventh-grade basketball squad. We had a new house a few blocks away from the school. The work paid well, dental and all, and the district dished out an extra stipend because I also helped with the ninth-grade football team at the high school down the road.

Those first few years, it felt like all the pieces had fallen into place. When the last bell of the school day screamed, students streamed into the hallways. I shared an office with the swim coach, a fat man named Bill Ringer. I'd kick up my feet, and he'd have his fat hand in a bag of Doritos. "Phil," he'd sometimes say. "It's not a bad life, is it?"

I had photos of Tammy on my desk, and I'd run my fingers across her face, asking the Lord how I landed on his good side. "It's not a bad life, Bill," I'd say. "Not at all."

I knew I couldn't just take it all for granted, so on Wednesdays I ran the prayer group for the athletes at school. The kids would pile into someone's living room, putting on the waterworks and telling us all how the Lord climbed into their hearts. We called the meetings Athletes for Christ. When I told Tammy about our first session, tears came to her eyes and she said, "I can't handle all that sweetness, Phil. It's just too adorable. Their itty-bitty hearts."

She could get sentimental like that, but who could blame her? I would watch the students recount their redemptions, every last detail of accepting Christ, and try to understand what was happening in their hearts. But that was a dream I woke up from before I could ever wrap my head around it.

"There he is, ladies and gents," Mike says. He has his phone camera running. "Say hello to Mr. Phil Turp."

I guess he's forty, forty-one. His red beard is unruly and looks like a burning jungle on his face. His eyes are big and wide, like a bug's. His arms run long and stringy. The sun has burned his skin hard and leathery. He gets my name wrong every time—it's *Tarp*—but I damn sure won't be the one to correct him.

"There he is indeed," Mike keeps at it. "The world's leading baby rapist, Mr. Phil Turp."

I bite on the filter of my Lucky Strike. "Still smoking, huh," Tammy says.

"Babe," I tell her. "I know, I know. I promised to quit. And I will," I say. "I'll quit smoking if it gets you back to me."

"You are crazy as hell, aren't you, baby killer?" Mike says.

"Hold on a second here, Mike," I say.

"Don't call me that. You don't know my real name. Trust me. You don't know shit about me. Not a damn thing."

"Well, what am I meant to call you, Mike?"

"PatriotVeteran1492, Turp. That's all you need to know."

"OK, Mike." I know I'm asking for it, but sometimes I can't help it. Working in the clinic, all you see are women sobbing, their men pacing around the waiting room. "Sorry, PatriotVeteran1492. Listen now, you've got me confused. In your mind, what is it I do to these babies, exactly?"

"Rape and kill," he shouts. He shoves his phone in my face. I guess my face is all over his Facebook again. "You do both."

I start toward the intersection, but Mike won't let up. He stamps alongside me.

"You are both. A rapist and a murderer. Both of them, you hear?"

"I hear you, alright."

The crosswalk flashes green in the shape of a mother walking a kid across the street. I start footing it to the other side. The sun is a sledgehammer.

"You do both, you son of a bitch," Mike says. "How do you intend to make right with the Lord when you finally croak?"

"S'pose the Lord will just have to understand that all I did was wipe a rag on a commode and push a mop." His face burns red—you almost can't tell where his beard ends and his cheeks start.

"Time to come clean, Phil," he says.

We are now standing in the middle of the street, and he pushes the phone camera so close to my face that it nicks my nose. I ball my fists out of instinct—I've got a thing about personal space. I could crack his cheekbone, maybe bust his eyebrow. But I take a couple slow breaths and shake my fists loose. He just won't give up.

"Get it all off your chest, Turp. How many baby rapes are you responsible for?"

A black Tahoe hums at the traffic light. The guy

behind the wheel snaps a photo on his phone. My face flashes hot. He's getting a real kick out of it, this guy in the Tahoe. I bet he thinks he's real slick. He keeps laughing his head off at me. I bet he's got himself a real nice wife back at home, maybe even a handful of kids running up and down the walls.

"Well, shit, Mike. Baby rapes, you say? I must've lost count."

"Don't talk to me. I don't talk to the devil."

"Wish I was the goddamned devil, Mike. I really do."

This confuses Mike. He cocks his head sideways.

"I'll tell you why, Mike. I can't imagine the devil has to stomach anyone quite like you down there."

Mike follows me to the blacktop rectangle where my pickup waits. Rust is eating away at the side panels, and the windows are lashed with scratches. I slide the key into the door and slip inside. The engine whines. Sometimes the battery cables come loose, but I'm getting tired. The last thing I want to do is go under the engine while Mike is hollering and filming me.

I try again and again, and the motor finally grinds to life. Mike walks alongside the pickup as I reverse. He puts his face so close it may as well be mashed to the glass. We meet eyes, and I see the red cracks across his. The AC coughs up hot air, but I leave the window rolled up. I throw it in drive and the pickup jumps as I slam my heel down on the gas. Mike gives chase in the rearview mirror. He waves an arm wildly. With the other, he's holding up his phone, still filming me.

Tammy's back in my ear—her breath blows hot on my neck. "You dumbass," she says. "He's got the license plate and all. He's going to find the home one day."

"Don't you worry about that. I won't let anyone hurt you, babe. You're always safe with me."

I cut right on 15th and Mike falls out of my rearview. I start thinking about the Bud Ice in the fridge at home. There's a can of chili in the cupboard, too. Then my mind hurtles each way. I think, That son of a bitch in the Tahoe must have real good air conditioning. I think, That son of a bitch, I bet he's got a woman who loves him. And then I'm thinking, How am I going to get right with the Lord?

"I don't know," I hear myself say. When I reach my neighborhood, a couple of boarded-up homes coast by. A crow lands on a phone line. Trash blows around in little cyclones. A broken toy sits in the street, but I don't see any kids around. "I just don't know," I hear myself say.

The first spring after we married, Tammy and I spent almost every weekend holed up in the house. We couldn't get enough of each other. We'd hold each other, our bodies glossed in sweat. We'd listen to mockingbirds sing. "You know mockingbirds can make just about any sound?" Tammy would say.

"Oh, yeah?"

"Those itty-bitty birds can mimic anything. You name it. They can creak like door hinges or bark like dogs."

And we tried for our first kid—sometimes two or three times a day. We lay tangled in bed for hours, trying and trying. Part of me knew the day would come, but I thought it was a long way off. I put on a real show, even kicked Wild Turkey for a couple months.

It was after our first visit to the fertility doctor. Tammy sat at the dining room table. She clenched her fists. She rubbed her eyes raw. The look on her face when I came home that day could've sliced right through me. "How long've you known?"

I stammered. I scanned my mind for any excuse, but I hesitated for a moment too long. "Long time," I said.

She fingered a strand of hair from her face and stared into a cup of coffee. "How long?" she said, but it didn't matter anymore. You can bury a lie like that, but one day it will show up again, ready to follow you around for the rest of your life.

The grass reaches my knees, but I am too tired for lawn work. I shoulder through the front door and head to the fridge. The first swig of Bud Ice hits me in the chest. I drop down on the couch but can't get comfortable. The house clicks and groans. My mind won't rest.

For a while after Tammy died, I slept in the pickup. My whole body ached and I woke to stray dogs howling every night. But I didn't know how to sleep inside, not without her.

After some time passed, I boarded up the bedroom door. I started coiling up on the couch each evening, the television playing all night. It didn't help—the morning it started, Tammy hovered right through the bedroom door. "Morning, Phil," she said. "What do you plan on fucking up today?"

I thought I was losing my mind, but she kept showing up, sometimes two or three times a day. I eventually took it as an opportunity, a chance to win back the woman I loved and lost.

"What're you looking at?" Tammy says now.

I tilt the phone so she can see. "It's Mike's Facebook page," I say. "He's putting me on there just about every day now. It's all baby killer this, baby killer that. Look here," I tell her. I point at the number of people following

Mike—five thousand. "These people get real worked up. I don't know why Mike doesn't bust someone else's balls. The doctor. Maybe a nurse."

"Well, it serves you right. You *are* a baby killer, kind of. Makes sense that thousands of people hate you."

"Tammy, love. You don't mean that." I reach out for her shoulder, but she floats off quickly.

A few posts down, Mike has already put up the video from this afternoon. The text reads, 'I THINK I LOST COUNT': TURP ADMITS TO MURDERING THE UNBORN. Nine hundred people have already liked it.

I toss my phone and watch it bounce off the far end of the couch. It hits the floor with a thud. I pop open a Bud Ice and light another Lucky Strike. Tammy leaves me alone with my thoughts, and I sit there for a long time. Smoke blooms and breaks apart. I am thinking, I know how I got here, but I just can't figure out why I had to be the one to get here.

It was early fall, a little more than five years ago. I was out on the porch. Sweat slid down my chest. I had my hands planted on my hips. I had just finished the lawn, and Tammy had rearranged the garage. We had spent months circling around it, but we finally made amends. I even floated the idea of adoption, and Tammy was starting to come around.

Tammy brought me a glass of water. She brought out a tray of water and ice cubes and all. A smile spread across her face. She kissed my cheek, and I knew we had turned a corner. But then the color left her face. She hunched forward and rested her arms on her knees. She wheezed. "Can you develop asthma this late in life?" she said.

The doctor said the cancer would spread fast. He said she would experience fatigue. Those first couple months, though, she couldn't sit still. She cleaned the kitchen twice a day. She disappeared into the attic for hours at a time. It was all nervous energy, but I mistook it for a sign of hope.

Kneeling next to the bed, she'd pray. "Please, Lord," she'd say. "Please, Lord. Please, Lord." And I understood it for the first time, how a desperate prayer could turn into a death wish, how the death wish could become just a prayer again.

Summer came, the grass yellowed, but it wasn't what you'd hope. The heat couldn't do anything for her. She started to writhe in bed. Her sweat came out cold. She whimpered in her sleep. When I cut the lawn, I could hear her moaning from inside, over the rumble of the mower's motor.

Her lungs finally gave out in August, and her parents hauled up from Waco. After they lowered her into the earth, her old man pulled me off to the side. "I was right," he said.

"Sir?"

"About you. You did right by her."

I could've sworn I heard Tammy scoff somewhere behind me, but there was nothing there when I whipped around. I turned back to Tammy's dad. "Thank you," I said. I was three quarters deep into a bottle of Wild Turkey, but even if you lived forever, you could never forget a moment like that.

I wake and drain a cup of coffee. The air conditioning only chokes out hot air, so I turn it off and stand around in my Fruit of the Looms until it's time to leave. I slip into my work pants and pause on the porch, looking at the abandoned houses across the street. Pigeon shit splatters on my pickup. A hot breeze wraps around me. I spark a Lucky Strike, and then smoke two more. I use electrical tape on the battery cables, then set off for work.

I spend the whole shift mopping floors, rooting around in the storage closet, and rearranging supplies for no real reason. I douse the clinic beds with disinfectant. The chemicals make my nostrils burn. I tell Tammy about the way my chest felt tight when I first saw her. I tell her I loved her that first moment. She calls me scum. I tell her I'm sorry and reach to touch her cheek, but she dissolves.

Around one o'clock, the receptionist interrupts my lunch break. That's okay—lunch today is three Lucky Strikes and a Dr Pepper. "Coach," the receptionist says. Her name's Carla, and she's called me that ever since I mistakenly mentioned I used to be a coach. I don't have the heart to tell her how much it hurts. For ten years, I wiped slobber from the special ed students' chins. I held the boys steady while they took a leak at the urinal. I wiped up the piss they sprayed on the floor.

"Coach," Tammy says, laughing.

"I *was* a coach," I tell Tammy.

"I know," Carla says. She smiles sweetly. "That's why I call you that."

"Yeah. What can I do for you?"

"Coach, there's not any chance you could cut the grass tomorrow, is there? The lawn care company dropped our account."

I press my teeth into the filter of a Lucky Strike. Sweat soils my work shirt. Things could be worse. "Well," I say. "S'pose I could."

"Thank you, Coach. Really."

"Sure," I say.

I pull the mower from the storage building. The grass isn't that tall. The problem is the perimeter of the lawn, the way it twists in sharp Z-patterns where the curb zigzags. They've also got these stone slabs spread out as a walkway across the lawn—a real nightmare to mow around. Tammy used to pull out a lawn chair and watch me mow our yard. "Excuse me, Mr. Lawn Boy," she'd joke. "But you missed a spot over there."

I'd tip the brim of my ball cap and say, "Sorry, ma'am," and then give her a little wink.

Right now, she's following me and saying how bad a job I'm doing. "You fuckin' this up, too?" she says.

Around the time I'm halfway done, Carla charges out of the clinic. She puckers her face, looking like she has something to tell me. She says there's a phone call for me inside.

"Must be a mistake," I tell her. I have no friends, don't receive phone calls.

"No," she says. "Not a mistake, Coach. It's someone from the FBI."

"Now I know you are pullin' my leg."

"I'm not, Coach. Really."

I tell her to take a message, that I will return the call. Someone is trying to get a laugh at my expense, and I don't have time for it. I mow until I finish up. I walk inside, wringing sweat from my shirt and toweling my face with a rag. There's a phone number jotted on a slip of paper in my workstation. I dial the number because I am curious, and a machine picks up—it really is the FBI.

"Carla," I say. I'm back into the reception area. "I'll have to get the weeds tomorrow. My stomach's in a bad way."

On the way out I pause under the vent and let the cool air roll over me. "Little morsels of relief, huh?" Tammy says.

"Don't even think about getting cute with me all the sudden," I say. "I just don't have time for it right now, Tammy. I really don't."

After the first DUI, the judge had granted me mercy, called me "a man bereaved." Community service and a thousand-dollar fine. No jail time, no suspended license. "I lost my wife to cancer, Mr. Tarp," he'd said. I thought he may've been crying. "I believe you are genuinely in need of a second chance."

But by the time I swayed back into the courtroom a second time, my shirt still sopping with Wild Turkey, all that sympathy had dried up. The way he spit out my name, I thought he would hurl the gavel at me. "Three weeks,

Mr. Tarp," he said, banging the stand. "That was all it took for you to squander the opportunity I gave you."

I did six weeks in county, playing cards with a guy who could only speak a few shaky phrases in English, all rehearsed. "I'm innocent man," he would say, flipping his deck to show his hand. He took me for my breakfast rations—two stale donuts the guard dropped off at daybreak—and a few Lucky Strikes every day. For a while, I considered him my only friend in the world. It was only after I got out that I read a newspaper article about him—he'd run over a kid, left him there to die.

I cut the steering wheel and swing down my street, still thinking about the phone call. The tires squeal. The pickup skids into the gravel driveway, shooting pebbles onto the lawn.

"A threat," the agent had told me. I pushed the receiver against my ear, thinking I misunderstood him. "A credible threat on your life."

"Mike isn't no threat," I replied.

"Mike? You mean PatriotVeteran1492. His real name's—"

"No, no. Don't tell me. Listen—Mike's just lost. Hell, we're all lost. Most days I look around and don't have the smallest idea where I am."

The agent paused, then cleared his throat. "Mr. Tarp, sir. I am talking about his followers online. I'm talking about guns. I'm talking about bombs."

"Bombs? Officer—"

"Agent," he corrected. "Surely you know abortion clinics have been bombed before, don't you?"

"OK, Agent. Look now. Me, I'm just a janitor. I clean toilets. I use a plunger. I man the mop. Don't anyone care that much about me."

"Bombs, Mr. Tarp. These folks believe that lizard people are running the country. They believe in shadowy cabals. They think the government poisons the tap water and it's turning the frogs gay. We're not talking about logical people, Mr. Tarp."

"Now, Agent. You mean to tell me lizard people and gay frogs plan to do me harm?"

"Mr. Tarp, I mean to tell you there are people out there who do not see the world the way we do. People who could target you with violence, and they don't respond to logic."

"You hear yourself, don't you? Logic, Lieutenant."

"Agen—" he started, but then gave up. He let out a raspy sigh. "OK, Mr. Tarp. As you like. You have my number when you need it."

"I appreciate that, but I can't see why I would," I said. The line clicked dead.

Later that night, I'm sleeping on the couch when the noises start. First a car screeches to a stop. Then, there's a powerful series of bangs, loud like gunshots. "Tammy, hon," I say. "I'm trying to sleep."

A brick crashes through the window, shooting glass all over the hardwood floor. My heart races, but I reach for an old beer on the coffee table and take a slug. The TV is humming. I stand up and slip into my house shoes. Another brick comes through the window, where the glass used to be. Tires shriek outside. I choke down another mouthful of beer, all suds. I tiptoe to the window. Outside, the weeds are overrunning the lawn. The street is silent and slashed with shadows.

It was the last day of summer break, and I hailed a cab outside county jail. The cop who booked me must have siphoned the twenty from my billfold, and the taxi driver told me to eat shit before he sped away. The mailbox was spitting up coupon books, warning notices from the city—the grass was up to my hips. I'd left the windows open on the night I'd been pulled over, and a summer rainstorm had the whole place smelling like soggy socks.

The next morning, I walked to Armstrong Middle School because my pickup was still impounded. I shouldered through the office door and saw Bill Ringer looking up at me as if he was laying eyes on a dead man. Doritos crumbs clung to the corners of his lips. Someone had shined my desk, and my photos of Tammy had disappeared. "Trying to erase me from your life, are you?" Tammy said.

"Tammy," I said. "I'd never. You're all I have ever wanted."

"Oh, Phil," Bill said. He looked at me with what I guessed was sympathy. "They took the pictures and everything else away in a cardboard crate. Earlier this morning."

"They took my shit?" I said.

"It's in the administrative office," Bill said. "I'm so sorry. I know you've had a hard go of it—"

"Best of luck, Bill," I said, and slammed the door before he could tell me how much he pitied me.

The assistant principal shot to his feet when I elbowed into his office. He offered his hand but recoiled when he saw my face. My fists were balled tight, my knuckles flashing white. I should have slugged him in his mouth. I should have kneed his gut and spit on his skull when he keeled over. I should have taken a handful of his blond hair and trawled him all the way up and down the hallways as the bell rang and the students swarmed out of their classrooms.

"Coach Tarp," he started. "I know this is difficult, but surely you understand."

I clenched my fists tighter and stepped toward him. But what good would it have been? I reached out, shook his hand, and said, "No hard feelings."

Thirty-five and booted from the only real job I ever had. You can't imagine how hard it is to find steady work when you've made a few mistakes. You can't imagine how tough it is to eke out a living, how badly they want to keep punishing you when you already want to hoist up the white flag and swing it and swing it and swing until your goddamn arms give out.

"That's it?" Tammy said. "That's all you've got?"

I tug the ripcord and the weed eater fires up. I go to town on the edge of the sidewalk in front of the clinic. Little grass trimmings sprinkle the pavement. Cars whiz past and I watch them. The sun slams down on me. When I finish lining up the lawn, I grab the larger weeds by their roots, tearing them out by hand. Earth is streaked across my shirt. The grass smells as fresh as a graveyard.

I'm so focused that I almost don't notice when Mike

appears on the corner. He has his mobile in his hand, trained on me like a sidearm. Tammy clears her throat, but I stop her before she can start in on me.

"No more. Not one more word. None," I say. "You're not my wife anymore."

"Your wife?" Mike says. He's moving my way.

"Not now, Mike."

"You're crazy as hell. Tell me, Turp. What *does* your wife think of what you do?"

"Mike, please." I can feel the blood hitting my brain.

"Is that why she left you? All the blood on your hands?"

Quick as a heartbeat I close the gap between us. Mike stumbles back, but I'm all over him. I open-palm him twice and scream, "Mike, Mike, Mike."

Mike turns to run. I snatch his collar, twist it until a cough rattles his chest. He falls down, face first. The ragweed floating in the air hits me. My eyes burn, start watering. Mike stammers. It all comes out in fragments. "Rape . . . Babies . . . You . . ." he says. "How many . . . Help . . . Please . . . Stop . . . Please."

The security guard, Ed, is in the front entryway to the clinic. Carla comes next. A nurse shows up behind her. The head doctor pushes to the front. For the first time, I notice a new banner strung up above the door: YOUR SAFETY IS OUR TOP PRIORITY.

Tammy glides up next to me, but I shoot her the bird. "Get the fuck out of here," I say. "And stay gone."

Carla presses her palms to her cheeks and mouths something I can't make out. The doctor hides his face behind a clipboard. "Mike, Mike," I shout. I turn to the group in the entry. "What happened to this man?" I hear myself shout. Who can say why, but I need to know. "Who hurt this man?"

Tammy is flying off down the street in a flash, her body flickering so that I can hardly see her. She's yelling something over her shoulder, but I can't hear a word she's saying, not anymore.

Mike, he's still down there on the ground. I squeeze every muscle in my body, trying to stop my fists from coming down on him, but they're anvils. Birds are barking, doors flinging open all across the neighborhood. Mike is saying through broken teeth, "We gotta get right with the Lord, Turp."

For the first time in years, everything is clear.

MAGIC

I asked my friend Donovan what we were building, but he told me to just shut up and keep working. He had me knocking scrap nails into PVC with a rusty hammer, attaching the piping to the wooden block that would become the base of whatever it was he had in mind this time. I scanned his backyard as I worked. It looked like they dumped their trashcan right there. A hot breeze rustled stomped-on Coke cans and sun-bleached beer boxes through patches of knee-high weeds. Something ripe wafted our way from the septic tank over in the corner, and I couldn't hardly focus. With the third nail I missed, Donovan said, "Lard Ass, am I gonna have to do this myself?"

I crouched and picked at a soggy strip of cardboard. The writing on it had faded and bled into a blur. I chucked the cardboard aside and a cluster of cockroaches broke apart, scattering each way like tiny soldiers trying to escape an ambush. I jumped back a step and Donovan laughed and stomped a few dead. Four, five years earlier my mom and dad had split and left my big sister and me high and dry. Our grandma took us in for a while. She was good to us and promised to be around forever, to even outlive us all. She would sometimes joke comparing herself with a cockroach. But cockroaches gave me the creeps, and my grandma died. A science teacher had once said that cockroaches had feelings—curiosity, excitement, fear, greed—but I couldn't stand them, the way they woke me each night in my bed crawling across my toes.

It was already early October, our first semester at the middle school, but the sun kept pounding the whole neighborhood, splitting small cracks in the sidewalk cement all along the streets. Donovan snatched the hammer from my hand and elbowed me aside. He started cranking the pipe, trying to find the right angle. Between his lips he had a Marlboro Light he'd pocketed from his dad's soft pack. "It's for a magic trick, Lard Ass," he finally said.

Donovan went wild for magic. He called every little idea he dreamed up a *magic trick*, just like that, even though you could find most of them in the middle school library, buried in the Scholastic Magazines they kept there or written about on science websites on their computers. I don't think either of us ever really knew exactly what point he wanted to make by blabbering about magic all the time, but he seemed to take pleasure in making sure you said he was right, whether you agreed with him or not. He stayed up all night reading online forums. Sometimes he slipped out into the alley and blew up a Coke can full of bathroom chemicals. Other nights he rigged a rocket and sent it roaring over the rooftop next door.

Donovan handed me the cigarette and said to take a puff. I pulled a lungful and coughed so hard we both had tears in our eyes, his from laughing. When I got upset about something, the few times I worked up the guts to talk back after he did something that lit my fuse, I told him his ideas were just science experiments. He'd say to shut my trap or kick me out. He could get like that, all bossy and hotheaded for no reason. When I slept over, he dished out directions like *light this* or *hold that*, *stand here* or *hide there*. He would brag about all his friends, people who followed directions better, but it was all talk: I was the only person who ever came to his house.

Most days I gave him no grief. I didn't want to work him up and get sent home. My big sister had become my legal guardian a few months earlier, after a car crash charred our grandma to a crisp, and she kept forgetting to restock our leaky fridge.

Donovan lived in a two-story home with paint scabbing off the sidewalls. Even though the wires crackled and the lights flickered, he thought he had a leg up on me because his place was planted in the same spot where it had been built. I lived in a drooping double-wide on the edge of the neighborhood, two streets over. Shacks and trailers lined either side of my blacktop road, but Donovan liked to remind me that ours was the only one that looked like it had survived a hurricane or two. Still, he was better than the other boys at school. They gave me the nickname Lard Ass. They were at that point in life when they had just begun to toy around with irony, and they got a real kick out of that. I had rails for arms and no real ass at all. Sometimes in the locker room, the boys thumped my ribs and laughed and asked shouldn't I be in a charity commercial for starving kids in some country no one knew how to pronounce. It was a cruel nickname that followed me everywhere, and even though he knew it stung me, Donovan had started using it whenever he got the chance. I didn't blame him for trying, but he'd never fit in with the other boys.

"Lard Ass," Donovan said now. He crouched and his hair fell down his pale cheeks in chunks, covering the acne scars on his face. “Pass me the nails, would you?”

We drifted through most of our afternoons like that. We met in the hallway after school, shoved our way through columns of classmates, and then soldiered through the sun back to his home, us both heaving and sour with sweat. His parents hunkered down on barstools at a dive down the road until long after the moon climbed up past the clouds. Me, I never had anywhere better to be. My big sister worked a graveyard shift at the Motel 6 near the highway, and Wild Turkey tucked her into bed each day before my school let out.

Donovan handed me the hammer and a bent nail, pointed to a spot on the pipe. “Put it there,” he said. I shuddered when a crow swooped down and cawed right past my head. For a second, I thought I was reliving it, the way my grandma sometimes slashed through my ceiling and soared around my bedroom. All shrouded in flames, she was not like I remembered her. At her funeral, my big sister and I swatted gnats from our faces as they lowered her into the earth. Wiping her eyes with a handful of her dress, my big sister kept forgetting the words to the prayers grandma had taught us, so I cupped her hand in mine and clamped down.

Donovan caught my wrist and stopped my hammering. He stepped back and surveyed the thing we'd created.

It weighed heavy to one side, looked like a crooked cannon. "You're going to love this," he said. "It's a great magic trick."

"I bet," I said. I just hoped he'd let me stick around for dinner. "What is it, exactly?"

I lumbered around in front of the contraption and watched as Donovan fiddled with it. He sprayed down the pipe a splash of some kind of liquid. He pulled a potato from his pocket and stuffed it down the tube. The sky burned purple and orange and clouds crept above us. The sun started to sag slanted beyond the silhouettes of homes stamped against the dusk.

When he punched my arm, I nearly stumbled. "Move," he said, just as I found my footing and hopped out of the way. The potato fired out like a bullet, busting through the fence, and tearing a big, jagged break in the boards. It opened to a spot in the next-door neighbor's backyard. A pit bull stuck his gnarled face through the gap and sniffed around, clenching the potato between its teeth. It growled at us from somewhere deep inside its chest.

"What the hell?" someone yelled from the far side of the fence. It was a man's voice, a gruff one. "What in the actual hell?"

I wrung sweat from the bottom of my shirt and stood around waiting for something to happen. Strange thoughts struck me in the heat. I felt like I'd lived my whole childhood that way, waiting for whatever came next. I saw my dad dashing to his drop-top Mustang, an old junkyard scrap job with different colored panels, and leaping into the backseat, my mother manning the wheel as the car screamed down the street and they disappeared forever. I saw grandma pinned under a ton of steel, flames scraping her skin away. I saw my sister signing the paperwork to drop out of her senior year in school, the grooves I'd never before noticed etched across her forehead.

The next-door neighbor's head came through the hole in the fence. Donovan ripped my wrist backward and dragged me toward the house. As he whipped me around, his cigarette fell in the weeds.

We collapsed on the kitchen floor. The doorbell dinged, and we plastered our palms to our mouths to stop the laughter. We were creeping to the foyer to get a peek through the peephole when the knocking began, heavy fists hitting the door. "Keep your fuckin' mouth shut," Donovan warned, but I had nothing to say. I imagined the wind gleaming the cherry on his cigarette out back. I could almost smell the sharp sting of burning wood, could almost feel the heat off the house as it became crackling ash.

Upstairs in Donovan's bedroom, we competed trading swear words. I earned extra points for having *Ass* in my name, but Donovan had the upper hand. He'd memorized a long list of words his dad drilled at the television screen when the Cowboys were losing. *Jizz rag*, *shit ass*, and *dumpster dick* gave him a solid lead. In my heart, I knew we shouldn't have said those words. I kept thinking about my grandma, how she'd have felt had she heard us.

A cockroach was scaling the wall above Donovan's bed. It had nearly reached the ragged crown molding when Donovan jumped up on the mattress and plucked it from the wallpaper. Donovan's eyes bulged like they did every time he had an idea. "Follow me," he said.

He darted down the stairs two at a time. In the kitchen, he said he had a magic trick that would make the potato gun look like a joke. We would freeze the cockroach in the freezer until it was good and dead, thaw it out, and then zap it back to life with electricity. He pinched the bug between his first finger and his thumb, its legs kicking about the same way grandma's used to when something was stealing her sleep. "Really my—our—best magic trick ever," he added.

"I don't know," I said.

"What's the matter, Lard Ass? You scared of

cockroaches?" He thrust the bug at my face and I sidestepped so quickly I nearly lost my footing.

"No," I started.

"Better watch yourself, Lard Ass." Donovan pushed the bug my way again. I slapped at it but missed. He was relentless.

"Okay, sure," I caved in. Maybe all that sun had stirred up my thoughts, but I had the hazy hope that we could determine whether death was really a done deal.

Donovan flung open the freezer door. He dug around in there until he found a spot and dropped the cockroach behind an ice tray. The bug busted its way up the drumstick of a Butterball chicken. We peeled off our shirts and slung them across a window unit coated in dust, let the freezer breathe on our chests. Donovan's arms hung stiff as stalks, slit with the glow of streetlights straining in from outside. He repeated that it would be our best magic trick ever, and I nodded. He dabbed a dirty dishrag on his head. I ran my palm across mine, tracing the scabs where my big sister had snipped my scalp while shaving away my hair. No more expensive haircuts, she had told me, meaning the five-dollar trims at Supercuts. She'd tugged a Bud Light from the cooler and rubbed the bottle along my skull.

I asked Donovan what next.

"We wait."

"How long?"

"An hour. Maybe two. As long as I say, Lard Ass. This is my house."

The cockroach tried to burrow its body in the frost built up in the freezer. Donovan yanked out a Hungry-Man TV dinner and lobbed it at me. "Microwave that," he said, and slammed the freezer door shut.

We divided up the TV dinner, meatloaf and mashed potatoes, while sitting cramped together on the couch. At school, I had taken to pocketing cafeteria food for later. I hadn't eaten this much at once since my grandma passed. Now I couldn't pace myself and choked down my share so fast my stomach tossed each way. Donovan scarfed down the whole desert, a brownie, in a single swallow, leaving behind only a few crumbs. When he went and took a leak, I licked the container clean, lapped it all up like a stray dog until I only tasted the wax coating.

The television hummed, but we didn't pay it much mind. We were busy arguing about raising the cockroach from the dead. We both agreed that yes, we could resurrect the bug, although we couldn't agree whether it would be magic that did the trick. When I told Donovan that science was why, his face flushed red and tightened and twisted. For a moment, I thought he might punch me, but then his face loosened, and he smiled in a way that made me suspicious. “Alright, I’ve got an idea,” he said.

He bobbed off to the bathroom and returned a moment later holding a can of Vidal Sassoon. He asked if I feared fire. I said no, but he already knew the answer. I’d already twice confessed to him how we couldn’t show grandma’s body at the funeral, the way blaze had gnawed off all her skin. “Well, don’t be a baby. It doesn’t hurt. I’ll show you,” he said.

The can hissed hairspray on his hand. He filled a bowlful of sink water and set it on the coffee table between cups filled with cigarette butts and crumpled paper towels. A man talked on the television screen, but the volume was low, and the old speakers rasped so that it all sounded like whispers. The rank of wet clothes, the stale cigarette smoke and nuked meatloaf, they all spun my head. Donovan plunged his fist in the water and steeped it there for a while. He grabbed a Bic lighter off the table. He flicked the flint wheel until a flame shot out, and I shrunk back into the couch. “Goddamn, Lard Ass. There anything you aren’t afraid of?”

Blue flames lashed from Donovan’s hand. He flapped it so close to my face I could feel the heat on my cheeks. I pulled away and thought of grandma. On the nights when she soared into my room sideways, she'd take a seat on the old chair in the corner of my bedroom, lighting a Pall Mall off one of the flames on her arm and staring me down. She never said anything, but the fire on her body burned so hot I'd wake tangled in sopping sheets.

"I can't feel a thing," Donovan said. He shook his hand until the fire faded away.

"That's a pretty good trick. You should do that in the science fair."

"Yeah," he said. I'd expected him to correct me. "Maybe I should."

He took my hand and doused it in hairspray. "Your turn."

I nodded and tried to think up an excuse to get out of it without him giving me too hard a time, tried to stop trembling, but he was already giving the Bic a few practice flicks. I asked if I should put my hand in water first. "Oh, no. You don't have to do that," he said.

"You sure?"

"Don't worry."

He sparked the lighter, inching it toward my palm, and the fire flared. A flame flashed around my hand, fingers and all. "I can't feel a thing," I said. I smiled and then the laughter clotted in my throat. Something sizzled sharp and my hand burned until it almost felt cold. The fire sheared off the top layer of my skin. As quickly as the pink bubbles formed on my knuckles, they blistered and burst. I couldn't find words. I swung my hand around hard trying to show Donovan something had gone wrong. He couldn't help himself. He leaned forward, laughing so hard he had to grab a handful of his stomach. "Okay, okay," he said between breaths. "Okay, okay."

"Shit, shit, shit," he now said. His eyes watered up and took on a soft glaze. From the panicked way he looked at me, I began to imagine my whole body blanketed in burn scars, so I buried it into the couch. When he reached for the bowl of water on the table, he knocked it over. "Shit, shit, shit," he repeated, and tore off toward the garage.

I crushed my hand into a cushion over and over until the flames finally fell away. The room stayed quiet for a few moments, and the ache in my hand seemed to have spread throughout my whole body. I couldn't think of anything to say. When I looked up, Donovan had a little fire extinguisher. "My dad keeps it in the garage," he said. His joints cracked as he shifted his weight from one foot to the next. "Because of the electricity."

In the kitchen, I ran faucet water over my hand for a quarter hour. A layer of skin had peeled away and what was beneath was bright and red. I shot down all of Donovan's ideas for my scalded hand. No hospital, I said. No milk.

No butter. No cream. He wrapped my fingers one by one and fixed the gauze in place with scotch tape. "You can go home, if you want," he said. "I'm sorry, you know."

I knew he meant it, but it didn't matter. "Just get the battery charger," I snapped, and for the first time since I met him, I knew I could hurt him.

With my good hand I pried the cockroach off a pint of Blue Bell ice cream. The freezer had left its body brittle and smooth to the touch. We planned to put it out on the porch for an hour, but even after dark, the heat shriveled it soft in a few minutes.

I swiped my good hand across the kitchen island and swept aside the TV dinner wrappers spread out everywhere. Strips of cellophane fell to the floor in a scatter, scrunched beneath the soles of our sneakers. "Plug that charger in, will you?" I told Donovan.

I decided to check for a pulse, the same way I push two fingers to my neck after grandma's night visits. Cockroaches have no necks, not really, so I settled for the bug's thorax. I couldn't find any signs of life. Donovan set up the battery charger, but the cord didn't reach. "Go get something that can reach," I told him, and he returned with an extension cord coiled against his chest like a snake. He unspooled it and placed the battery charger on the island. I ran my pinky along the surface, moving the roach around to make sure it was still dead.

"Get ready," I said. "Back up."

I pressed the wires to either side of the cockroach's torso. Nothing happened. "Crank up the power."

Donovan dialed up the notch on the charger and I shocked the bug three times. "More," I said. I could hear the dog next door bawling its heart out.

"Take it all the way up," I said. The cockroach startled, flipped, and landed on its backside. Its little legs kicked as if it had come back, but death was still chasing it.

"Is it alive, Lard As—?" Donovan began, but he shirked back when I shot him a look. The cockroach's legs wiggled. I turned it over onto its feet and it took a step, and then another. It walked three inches, maybe four. I wondered if it felt alive, or maybe something like hope.

But then it stopped. I lowered my face to it and couldn't see any movement. I tapped it, but it appeared almost serene, it was so still. "You try," I ordered, and Donovan couldn't flick it back to life either. I zapped it four, five, six times, over and over until a faint finger of smoke fluttered up from its body. Its legs had melted to the tabletop.

Donovan's dad exploded into the house, knocking

over a vase as Donovan's mom flailed in behind him. Donovan fumbled for the mess spread out on the island. "We gotta hide this," he said, but I clutched his wrist, wrestled it down. I felt every twitch in my body, the scabs itching my scalp, my heartbeat pulsing down into my burned hand.

Donovan's dad whistled his way into the kitchen. He popped the top off a Coors Light. I took hold of Donovan's shoulders and jerked him back and forth. "Do it, Donovan," I said. "Do the magic. Bring it back to life."

"Everything alright, boys?" his dad slurred. He was looking at the cockroach on the table. "What the hell happened here—"

I waved him away. I wrapped my arms around Donovan and drew him in closer. "Just do the magic, shit dick," I said. "Be a fuckin' magician, you cunt rag."

"Whoa, whoa, hey now—" said Donovan's dad.

I shut him up with a raised hand and swiveled back to face Donovan. I hugged him, pulled him in tight, squeezing until he coughed. "Do it now, you cum dumpster."

RENT MONEY

James is all worked up again, waving his gun and acting like he gives a damn. Raising his voice. Pacing the kitchen. Insisting Theresa will do just fine. Saying he believes in her, that she's stronger than before, that she'd be doing a good thing for their family. But he's running his fingers through his hair the way he does when he's nervous. He snatches a beer from the fridge and pops the top. Worried he'll wake the kid, Theresa cuts her eyes at the baby monitor. "Took me an hour to get him down," she says.

Not listening, James sits across from her at the kitchen table and tips back the beer till the can's empty. Burps. Crushes the can. Snarls his face. He starts speaking even faster than before, hardly takes a breath between each word. Waves his arms like he's flagging down an emergency vehicle. "You'll get the job done, I know it," he says.

"Thanks, hon," she says, but she isn't so sure. Part of her suspects he thinks she'll shit the bed again. His words last time—*shit the bed*—when she came back empty handed. She drove all the way to the apartment complex on the other side of the train tracks, but she couldn't collect. Saw James's tenant—a woman three months behind on rent—carrying a baby in her arms. Theresa never got out of the car. Curled up in the driver seat. Cried 'til her eyes ran dry and burned.

James is sinewy but soft, the way some alcoholics are. A small belly that bounces when he moves about. He's forty-one, eighteen years older than her, but he sometimes makes her feel like the only adult in the house. When they married five years back, he promised a clean, simple life. He drove her away from the shotgun shack where she grew up, away from a lifetime of Welfare oatmeal at each meal. She'd spent seventeen years falling asleep to the sound of whimpering, the strays her mother had taken in, and waking to find the flea bites on her ankles rubbed raw and bloody.

James is back on his feet now. He stamps around the kitchen, flinging open the cabinet doors and revealing their guts. The sippy cups, the plates decorated with cartoons, the baby bottles. Theresa can't help but wonder if he picks these particular cabinets to make a point.

Theresa's sure James knows she doesn't like the idea, but she also knows he doesn't know what else he's meant to do. He sometimes asks her how he's supposed to feed a wife and a child when his tenants don't live up to their end of the bargain.

Theresa sighs and James shoots her a stern look. "I'm just tired," she tells him, and it's true. Between the baby and back-to-back doubles at the bar, she's hardly slept the last two days. "I'm sorry."

James says nothing. He jerks open the fridge and fishes out another beer, popping the top. He chokes down the whole can in a couple swigs, and then slips a little silver flask from his pocket and tips that back, too. Shivers a little as the whiskey goes down.

As much as she wants to, Theresa doesn't bring up the booze. James is supposed to have kicked alcohol a month ago. He made a big show of it, dumping the last case of Miller High Life bottle-by-bottle into the toilet. Theresa stood at the living room window and watched him lug a sack of liquor bottles down to the curb. Smiled as he tossed the bag into the big brown trash can, turned toward the house, and saluted somewhat sarcastically, marching back up the drive. Felt good—he saw things her way for the first time in months, years maybe. A week later, she came back from a closing shift at the bar, opened the fridge, and found two twelve-packs on the bottom shelf. "But I *am* clean," he protested. "I'm only drinking beer."

Theresa has known drunks from day one. Her mother drank a box of Wal-Mart wine each night. Her father, shacked up with another woman two towns west, polished off a fifth of Famous Grouse each day with dinner. And James, who'd long since ditched his two-drink daily max, now drank High Life every day. A six-pack, at least.

Still, she managed to convince him to kick, even if he only lasted a week. He understood her point, that it was for their boy's sake. It felt powerful, her guilting him over what happened. Meant to be babysitting while she tended bar, he'd slipped out and left the kid home alone. Tied one on down at the Harbor Point. Telling stories with the old vets. They all think James's a saint, a war hero. A high kill count in Nam—more than a hundred communists, he'd swear. A Green Beret with clandestine missions in Cambodia, or wherever it is that's next to Vietnam. But he'd been a weekend warrior, National Guard, had never served in any war, and when Theresa got home, the boy was in the backyard with a snakebite on his calf.

A garter snake, she guessed. Could've just been a scratch, actually, but still. Either way, there was a snake nearby. The boy'd crawled right through the dog door—it came with the house—and got bit. Just two years old.

"You'll need the gun," James says now.

"Is that really necessary?"

"Yes, it's really necessary."

Theresa looks her husband over. His black hair plugs. His flashy watch. The shiny silver buckles on his leather shoes, seventies style. It drives her nuts, having to admit the truth to herself: If she'd met James now, and not when she was seventeen, he'd be the kind of guy she'd laugh at from across the bar.

She's thinking it, so she just says it: "You're so worried I'll mess up, why don't you go over there and collect the rent yourself?"

James sits again. He straightens his back, cranks his neck to either side, makes fists of his hands. When he finally says to shut up, Theresa shuts up.

"Just zoom over to the apartment," he says. "You flash the gun. She coughs up cash. Simple. You show no fear. None. These people feed off your fear. You walk off and make sure you don't give the other tenants enough time to lose their shit."

"But—"

"But what? She's already two months behind on the rent."

James takes hold of her hand, squeezes it white.

Speaks so fast Theresa can hardly follow. He pauses, sucks in a deep breath, and says, "What do you think? Piece of cake, right?"

Theresa feels a sigh trying to come up, but she swallows it down, frustration and all. Only nods. Somewhere in her heart she knows the snakebite was the final straw. But she can't just leave. Besides, she still thinks James can change. And if he doesn't, all she needs is another final straw.

James pulls the pistol from his waist. Slides it across the table. "This is all you need," he says. "Simple, simple."

Theresa just wants the conversation to end. She places the pistol in her purse, tries to convince herself it'll be easy. James goes to the fridge for another beer. While his back is turned away, she snatches the baby monitor and drops it in the purse. Stupid, yeah, but she needs a reminder of what's at stake.

"You know, we all have responsibilities," James says. "We all have troubles, sure, but we all gotta pay our bills. It's a matter of being honest. Responsibility is about honesty, and truthfulness matters."

Yeah, yeah, James, Theresa thinks. How about those hair plugs? Those honest? And what about renting out slum apartments to meth monsters? That how you honor your responsibilities to your wife? To your kid?

"Get a move on, yeah?" James says.

"This is the last time."

James smiles. A big, satisfied smile. "You must really love me, don't you?"

"Sure, I love you," Theresa says. And she does. Just like a gunshot victim loves a bullet too dangerous to remove.

Their marriage wasn't always like this. James wasn't always like this. When he strolled into Night Town the first time, Theresa was two months out from her eighteenth birthday. The club was popular with a certain crowd. Drunks and cokeheads. James looked the part, but he came off differently. He said please and thank you. Tipped thirty percent. While the others sniffed themselves stupid in the shadows, Theresa never saw him do drugs. Never even served him more than two bourbons in a night. Sometimes he didn't even finish the second.

By their first date, James was already somewhat of a regular at the club. Had come in six or seven times. They were sitting in his car, a souped-up 'Vette, '85. "Where are your people from?" he wanted to know.

"Here," she said. Meaning North Texas. "You know—the area."

"Beautiful place," he said.

"Is it?"

They laughed together. The whole region was flat, an endless field decorated with strip malls and highways. Flatlands beneath boring clouds all the way north to Oklahoma.

"And you? What town did you watch fade in your rearview?"

"A place so small it hardly deserves a name. In Alabama. An hour or so outside of Birmingham."

"Oh, so you're a real country guy."

"Tent revivals and bingo halls, the whole deal."

"We just play the part here, but we're city people."

Later, James dropped Theresa off outside the shack, and a swarm of dogs shot out from the open garage. Dashed straight to the passenger side. Jumped and barked until she rolled down the window and petted them.

"That's a lot of dogs y'all got," James said.

Theresa smiled in a way closer to wincing. "Orphans, sort of. My mom takes in every stray in the neighborhood. She can't hardly feed us, but she cooks rice and beans for those dogs every day."

"Hm. Sounds rough."

"What's rough are the flea bites."

"Yeah?"

She rolled up her sock. Little bitemarks circled her ankle. Scratched raw and scabbed and scratched raw again.

Bubbled yellow with puss. "The old lady loves them," she said. "Makes me and my sisters cook them meals. All we're allowed to eat is the oatmeal."

"Oatmeal's not so bad."

"Ever tried Welfare oatmeal?"

James looked up at the shack. The wooden outer walls shed paint like dead skin. The roof sagged in the center. The shape of an old woman, slumped and shadowed, stood in the window.

He said, "If I'm out of line, just say, but . . ."

"But what?"

"Why don't you stay at my place tonight?"

The 'Vette backed down the drive, flicking up gravel on either side. Theresa looked in the rearview. James turned and they passed the old birdfeeder mailbox and knocked-over trash cans. James hit the gas and the car shook over a pothole. Theresa looked up. Watched the old shack fade in the rearview.

Theresa whips the Kia right on Park Avenue. She's in no hurry to get where she's going, but to hell with the NO RIGHT ON RED sign. Reeboks sneakers dangle from a power line. Like her boy's but bigger. The clouds turn gray, gather above in bulbs. The pistol is in her purse on the passenger seat. Can't weigh more than a pound or two, but it may as well tip the car on its side, heavy as it weighs on Theresa.

Flashes of sunlight hack through the dusk, flicker low in the distance. Shacks speck the horizon. Shadows shifting shapes. Theresa eases up on the gas. Coasts past Hilltop 24 Liquor. She guesses the name's ironic.

A bunch of winos quiver in the parking lot. Streetlamp light shivers on the street surface. Theresa swings into the parking lot and the baby monitor spills out of her purse, clunks on the floorboard. She reaches over. Puts it back in the purse. The Kia fits nicely between two parked pickups. One has a bumper sticker with a photo of a crying baby boy. IF HE'S NOT ALIVE, WHY KILL HIM? it says.

Theresa steps out and a wino starts sauntering her way, swaying his head to either side. He clears his throat. Looking him over, she guesses he's around twenty-five, twenty-six.

"I can't help you," Theresa says. Likes to cut them off before they start in on her. Besides, she's here to beg, too.

"Lady," the wino says, but Theresa turns away.

"Lady," he shouts. Cicadas rattle all around. He raises his voice. "Lady."

Drunks just don't know when to quit, she thinks. She walks across the parking lot, stepping on the weeds pushing up through the pavement. "Lady, please," the wino says, but Theresa isn't listening. Her heartbeat in her ears. Ready to show James what's what.

She stops and checks the number. Unit 105. Ready to kick down the door. Remembers the pistol back in her purse. Someone's moaning in the apartment, a throaty moan, equal parts wounded and pleasure.

Theresa starts back to the Kia. Laughs to herself. Thinks, Boy, am I going to feel bad interrupting whatever's going on in there.

Theresa knows the point when it happened, when it all changed. It was two years after they'd married, the marriage the outcome of a whim-of-the-moment trip to the county courthouse. Sounded like a good idea on their sixth date.

James never had a problem making money, even if his ideas weren't always straight. He knew how much security mattered to her. She'd told him more times than she could count, the way her mother used to blow her entire Navy pension on the strays and wine. James always had a plan. One scam ran out of steam and he already had the next lined up. Spent a couple years selling low-cost chemicals for big prices to cleaning companies. A year in telemarketing. But after he got the idea to buy a slum apartment and started losing cash hand over fist, Theresa couldn't help but look back and think that she should have fought it more.

"It was a sure-fire deal," he said.

"Then why'd it go wrong?" she said.

"It wasn't in my hands."

"Then whose hands was it in?"

And Theresa knew it, she knew how much people changed when they felt pinched, but it still came as a surprise when James raised his fist for the first time. Told herself it was a one-time incident. Before James, she had only known three types of men: those who groped her at the club, those who treated her like jailbait and kept a wide berth, and those who hit. James had now turned out like the rest of them.

The first time he had her drive to the apartment complex, she parked in the liquor store lot. Tried to coach herself. An hour later, she was still sitting behind the wheel. Coiled up in the seat. Crying.

"This is the last time you come back without cash," he said. She knew he could talk big sometimes. Also knew he meant it this time.

A truck passes, sprays up puddle water. Soaking, Theresa listens to her shoes squish in the damp grass. Crosses the street, makes toward her car.

The wino is still there. Has a wino buddy now. Together, the two huddle between her Kia and the pickup next to it. The Kia's passenger door is wide open. Wino number one fiddles with something. The clouds are clogged with rain—Theresa smells it.

The first wino crowds Theresa. She tries to push him off, but while she's distracted, his wino buddy snatches the keys from her hands. Wino number one takes the pistol from her purse. Theresa thinks, A pistol seems a hell of a lot bigger when it's shoved in your face.

She could cry, but what comes out is much worse: She asks if either wino has kids.

"Yeah," wino number one says.

"What? Yes," his buddy adds.

"They as worthless as y'all?"

"Lady, fuck yourself," wino number one says.

She knows it sounded bad, but she didn't mean it that way. Just needs to know if shitbag parents could only give birth to shitbag kids.

The wino cuts the Kia left on Malcolm X. Shouts something drunk out the window. Theresa's purse flies out. Flips, hits the grass, and falls open. Sends the baby monitor somersaulting.

The door opens and Theresa swings the baby monitor hard as her arms allow. Nails the woman on the face, sends her back-first to the floor. Theresa steps over the tenant, straddles her, sees her brow, busted open and bloody. The woman is snorting and sucking air, shocked. The room smells of sex and sadness. A man snores loudly in the bed. Never so much as flinches. All Theresa can see of him are his ankles. Hairy, white flesh jutting from the sheets.

"Fuckin' winos," Theresa says. She sets off on foot—the walk home will take an hour, maybe more. She thumbs through a wad of cash, says, "Fuckin' meth monsters."

Shadows paint the street, the shape of trees. Theresa lies on her front lawn, hugs the baby monitor to her chest. Pulls it close to her ear and holds her breath. Listens to James stomping around inside. The blinds slit open. Light spilling out on the grass.

James is coming, but shadows give her cover. She pulls a hundred from the cash, stuffs the rest in the mailbox. She's got her mind on somewhere. Doesn't know where exactly.

Theresa starts off down the street. The wind picks up, murmurs through the leaves. She keeps the baby monitor held to her ear. Hears now the soft wheeze of her boy's sleep. James bursts out into the lawn. Waving his arms all over. Flashing the flashlight up and down the street. Theresa dives onto the grass past the curb. She'll wait him out. When he's drunk and asleep, she and the boy will set out, watch the town shrink in the rearview, windows down and breeze biting their faces. She'll find work, find a way to make rent money. She shrivels as small as she can. Squeezes her eyes shut as the flashlight glow crawls her way, stretches out its fingers and grabs at her.

SCREAMING EAST ON I-10

I just want to get home, but home's never quite where I left it. After work tonight, I glide along the streets of Simi Valley, nearly nodding off a time or two, in search of the complex where I stay. I almost crashed once before, at the tail end of the twenty-hour trek from Texas, when Hank appeared in my passenger seat. I left home to get away from him, but there he glimmered, the same guy who taught me exactly how much to water down Ma's wine bottle when we snuck a glass. He's next to me again now, in my periphery, smog hovering above the seat, but when I glance over, there's only emptiness. I yank the wheel straight just in time to miss a Pinto parked on the shoulder.

I hook a left on Royal. My bones ache something awful. Eight hours of hauling pallets off Mack trucks behind the T.J.Maxx. Lugging boxes back and forth, crates of jeans with mismatched pockets, shirts with sleeves of different lengths, lampshades with small tears in the material, beauty products suspiciously near the expiration date. Sneaking off to suck down Parliaments in the chute of the industrial trash compactor at the back corner of the warehouse. The manager hollering at us to shape up or ship out. Demanding to know if he pays us to drag ass all shift long. But it's my lucky night: I chewed up a couple pills some poor bastard dropped near the conveyor belt and itched my nose all the way back to the breakroom to clock out.

I moved west to get away from Ma. She became difficult after Hank, talked about death all the time, washed and folded Hank's old clothes like he was going to stumble out of his bedroom one day searching for clean socks. For three years, everything was *a mother's grief* this, a *lost soul* that. You'd think she forgot she still had a living, breathing kid. I didn't want to think about death, about Hank. I didn't want to waste away taking care of someone who wouldn't take care of me back. I drove half the country looking for somewhere I didn't have to consider whether death is the end. But Hank trailed me like a shadow. It didn't help that I landed here in a townhome with roommates who couldn't help but remind me of the day I found him. He had stone limbs, a stiff face. A phone charger choked around the crook of his arm, foam filling the cracks between his teeth.

It's like our complex moves a couple streets every time I go to work or step out to buy smokes. The management company named it Creekside, but if you do a lap or two around the parking lot, see what kind of people rot away on plastic lawn chairs next to their front doors, you won't bother asking why everyone calls it Tweakside. After a half hour of wrong turns, I cruise through the front gates—they've been broken since I moved here, maybe never worked—and felt the brief satisfaction of a small victory.

Our townhome isn't much, a two-bedroom unit with hardly enough space to fit the four of us. The place makes everything feel temporary—the thick green shag carpet with loose seams and inexplicable bumps, no photos or posters on the wall. At any moment, someone could come along and strip the place bare, and no one would know anyone had ever been there. We've tacked up old, stained T-shirts as curtains, and the towels we bunched up in a mound to catch water leaking off the AC unit have lately started to breathe a sharp rot. We're all around eighteen or nineteen, but life's decay has left us thin-limbed and miserable.

I've got my mind set on some shut-eye, but just as I

shoulder through the front door, a meat cleaver hums across the living room like a gigantic gnat, drilling into the wall. Drywall shoots all over the carpet, little white flecks in the shag, and the spot around where the cleaver's stuck in the wall is all wounds. Holes where poorly tossed knives have gnashed it up. My roommates can't help it—they are drawn to small acts of destruction like a moth to a bulb. When they tie one on, they can keep it up all night.

Face nods at me, smiles a mouthful of teeth like crumbling headstones. When he grins, his eyes and nose twist up tight, and you get the feeling he can hardly handle whatever goes on between his ears without making a joke out of it.

"Hey, Tex." His voice's a house fire. A year has passed since I watched dust blot out Dallas in my rearview, but he still hasn't thought up a better nickname.

P.A. sits up on the couch, claps for the performance. "Great toss, Face." When he speaks, you can see the empty slot where he lost a tooth in a brawl with a bartender he shorted or a woman he did wrong, I can't remember which.

Face's girlfriend is on the other side of the couch, pale and hollow, rocking either way with her knees hugged hard against her chest. She was probably normal once, or whatever passed for normal, but life's done a real number on her. Face says she looks like someone left her outside too long.

"Hey, Face." I survey the room, the chunks of wall on the carpet, the small pile of knives. "What are y'all doing?"

"Well." Face clasps his hands like he's making it all simple for a child. "We're just throwing knives at the wall."

"I can see that much." We pawned all the landlord's cutlery weeks ago. "But where'd you get the money for new knives?"

Face ignores me, lobs another one that sticks in the wall. P.A. grunts some kind of guttural approval. "What a throw."

His real name is Justin, but he got his nickname because he comes from Pennsylvania. After he got caught pushing pills at an N.A. meeting, his old man sent him packing. To hear P.A. recount it, his father's decision was deeply unfair because, after all, the pills were actually just diuretics he'd pocketed at the Walgreens. P.A. points a slim finger, yellow as nausea, at the cleaver lodged in the wall. "Let another one rip. That was pure luck."

Face's girlfriend snags a crumpled pack of Parliaments from inside her bra, fires one up. She works the register at a Wendy's and has a real name, but I never have learned it. I only know her by the nickname Face cooked up for her: Minimum Wage Mama.

Face winds up again, steak knife in hand. The lights flicker, lash us. I'm still counting holes in the wall when the next knife hits handle-first and ricochets across the carpet. Face licks his finger, holds it up, and laughs. "Must be the wind."

Face got his own nickname a long time ago, years before I wandered west. The way he tells it, his friends gave it to him in middle school because looking at him made them want to hack up their last meal. I've never heard a guy shit on himself like that, but nothing much seems to bother Face. He wears his shame snug as skin, laughs if unsettled kids stare at him when we go out. This is a nice town, health food stores and strip-mall churches, gentle, green mountains fencing it all in. Still, something's off about the place.

P.A. tosses up his arms, howls. "You shit the bed on that one, Face."

Face makes a fist, shakes it. "Let's see you do any better."

But P.A.'s had enough. He lays his head on the armrest and drops into a deep sleep, snoring from the start.

Face grabs a light bulb from the kitchen counter, pitches it hard at P.A. It shatters against the windowsill behind the couch, sending a spray of shards everywhere, but P.A. doesn't flinch. Minimum Wage Mama springs to her feet, shouts. "We need that you moron."

"We've got plenty." His voice is full of indignation, shock that she can't see a plain fact. He climbs on the counter, unscrews the kitchen light bulb, and the room goes a shade darker. He makes a big show of it, guts the bulb, and crushes little crystals into it. He'll do anything for crank—I've seen him chug curdled milk on a bet, choke down rotten eggs, eat a bug plucked from the carpet. He once housed a six-pack of energy drinks because we promised him a hit, but we had already finished off the sack. He spent the rest of the night knotted up on his naked mattress, now and then vomiting into a plastic grocery sack.

Right now, he sucks in a lungful, holds it until his face hardens. He exhales a small smog and offers me a beer, an Olde English. "Because you're a good guy, I don't mind giving this to you free of charge."

"Thanks." I swat away smoke. I bought the case and stocked the fridge last night—neither Face nor P.A. have jobs or money—but what use is pointing that out?

Before I packed up and left Texas, Ma warned me

to stay safe in California, but she said it as if reciting a prompt. "There are riots out there."

I told her all that finished years ago. I had no idea whether that was true. I just wanted her to tell me to stay, that she'd get a grip on herself. "I'm more likely to die in a wildfire."

"You'll be fine."

Then, she stood barefoot in the gravel driveway in front of our trailer, hacking her way down a cigarette, and shriveled in my rearview mirror.

P.A. glimmers as his chest rises and falls. Minimum Wage Mama flicks away tiny fragments of glass from her bare thighs. She can't get comfortable. She keeps squirming, and something's buzzing beneath her.

I point her way. "Your phone. It's vibrating."

She doesn't hear me, or if she does, she doesn't show it. Face passes her the bulb, and she sucks a small wraith of smoke through the straw. After a while, she stares at me. "I ever tell you about my kid?"

"No." I already know the whole story, sure, how her kid, a little boy, has a deadbeat for a dad. "I don't think you have."

Sob story or not, Minimum Wage Mama can't hold my attention. The more she talks, the less I hear. I think of Ma, of Hank. I down half my Olde English in a few big slugs that ache my chest. When I look back, I notice Minimum Wage Mama's clothes. I raise my hand, stop her mid-sentence. "Is that my shirt?"

But when I glance around, they are all wearing my clothes, Minimum Wage Mama and Face and P.A.

"How should I know?" She shrugs like I asked her whether God exists. "I got it from your room."

Someone passes me the bulb. I shake my head no but take it anyway, and after a hard hit, hand it off again. I push aside a T-shirt curtain, finger a gap in the blinds. Night bruises the sky purple. An ambulance cries out somewhere far off. For a flash, my head fills with images of bodies busted into pieces, people begging for help, bystanders phoning 911. Truth be told, Minimum Wage Mama's nickname doesn't sit right with me. Back in Texas, Ma makes minimum wage at the bar she tends.

The crank sets in. Something smashes into the wall. Someone lights a cigarette, and just as I turn to ask for one, Face gifts me a lit Marlboro Red. The smoke sears my lungs, but I can't enjoy it. The buzzing's started up again, and my nerves are razors.

Last time I talked to Ma, she spoke with the loose drawl she took on whenever she got around half a bottle deep. I was on break at work, sipping a Keystone Light at the pay phone and watching wildfires shave the mountaintops bald. I knew she was hurting, but why couldn't she just, say, ask me to come back?

"Bet you're doing well for yourself out there."

"It's not like they make it out on TV."

"Bet you're glad to forget about us."

"What are you even saying?"

Face falls into the spot on the couch between me and Minimum Wage Mama, gives me a soft punch in the ribs. "You good, Tex?"

"My ma wants me to come home." The words taste empty.

"No one ever asks me to come home." Face laughs something sad and forced, but resentment's in there too. He claims he was raised by foster parents and has real bad stories, stuff you see on the news. He's also the best bullshit artist I've ever met. Still, I'm never quite sure, so whenever he sometimes wakes me up rifling through my pockets, I only say something if he snatches a big bill off me. Who knows? Maybe his foster dad really did rip out Face's toenails for sneaking out, like he says, maybe not. Either way, it's hard to get all that mad at a guy like that, someone who's never had a home at all.

Face gets back to his feet, points at the blades all in a pile on the carpet. He grabs a potato peeler off the kitchen island and hurls it at the ceiling.

The couch cushions shiver. "What is that *buzzing*?"

Minimum Wage Mama cuts me a face full of hate, red and crumpled. She says no one has a single clue what I'm talking about. She says why don't I get a doctor to check my ears. She says why don't I just shut my fucking trap already.

A few dozen throws later, the landlord blasts through the door, a shock to all of us because he normally stays shacked up at his old lady's.

Minimum Wage Mama leans toward me. "Listen: My kid just needs a good father figure."

"Like Face?" I ask, but it's hard to hear over the landlord's shouting.

I swivel his direction. "John, man. Long time."

"That's not my name."

"Well. What was it again?"

"You're fucking hopeless."

I'm not so arrogant I can't admit when someone's got a good point. "Right, right."

P.A. snores through the whole thing, occasionally twitching.

Minimum Wage Mama taps my shoulder. "Like Face, yeah. You think he'd maybe make a good dad?"

I look Face's way, see him taking another draw off the

bulb. I shrug. How can you blame her for wondering? I know desperate when I see it. Besides, my old man must have seemed like a fine father until he hauled off with a woman my ma called “his new slice of ass,” her voice vaulting each time she brought it up.

“Sure.” I turn to Minimum Wage Mama. Then, something P.A. told me comes to mind, how he once went out to the desert with Face and witnessed him gutting a baby fox with a stick, stirring its innards.

The buzzing’s at it again. It gets me thinking of the way the TV hummed when I found Hank. Since he died, it’s felt like I’m facing down a brutal wind with no skin on my body at all. He was my big brother. Now, he’s just a boxful of bones a few feet beneath the topsoil. I don’t mean to, but I huff. “Can’t you just turn your phone off?”

Minimum Wage Mama launches to her feet, stalks straight back to the bedroom.

Face shakes his head. “It’s her kid, Tex.”

I scan the room, peek out the blinds. “Where?”

“The buzzing. Her kid’s calling. I think she forgot to leave him grub. But you’re right. Don’t know why she doesn’t just turn the fuckin’ phone off.”

“I guessed as much.” Sadness twists my intestines. Truth is, I’d have never expected a thing like that in a thousand years.

John smacks his hands together, a loud, angry clap. "You guys hear me?"

Regret falls on Face like a shawl. "John, I'm sorry, man. What were you saying again?"

"Get the hell out." He swings the front door open, lets it slam against the wall. "You're evicted, all of you."

"Says you and what army?" But when he steps my way, fists balled, I shirk deep into the couch cushions.

P.A.'s head pops up. "Y'all hear someone taking a leak upstairs?"

I kick him in the ass. "Keep it down, man. Minimum Wage Mama's trying to nap back there."

Face snatches a cockroach from the floor, slips it between his lip and teeth like chaw.

"I mean it." John squeezes the telephone in his hand. His knuckles go white. I rub my eyes hard, and by the time the room takes shape around me, he's already dialing the cops.

I look back from the door, see the landlord on his knees in front of the knife pile, swaying as if he can pray away what happened to his place. I can't find any words, not a goddamn one of them. When I head out in the parking lot, a hot breeze running over my body, I hear P.A. dragging his heels behind me.

Not long before sunrise, P.A. sits up in the passenger next to me in my pickup. The first morning light glows his veins bright blue. He left his window cracked, and gnats buzz all around us. He's thinner than last night. A strong enough wind could shred him to pieces. He digs a finger deep in his nose, yawns. "Still roommates."

I look at the Cinemark parking lot where we slept parked. Wind tosses wrappers here and there. A rat runs past, a shadow chasing it. "Still roommates. Say, did we ask John about the security deposits?"

P.A. slaps me on the shoulder. "That's good shit, Tex."

I get out, pad over to a pay phone. Ma doesn't pick up.

Back in the truck, I drowse away. Time passes—ten minutes, two hours, I can't say. A hardnosed cop jolts me awake, tapping the window. "You can't sleep here."

I see right through him all of a sudden. "You're not a real cop." He's just a security guard, a cheap, plastic badge tagged to his shirt. Still, his eyes burn me alive. He lifts a baton, whirls it.

The pickup starts on the second try. Out of the parking lot, a few minutes down the street, the cab shakes as we rattle over train tracks. We push on to wherever we're headed. A mountain rises over the valley ahead. Wildfires claw all about its face.

I pull over at a gas station, hit another pay phone. No luck.

We drive for an hour, circling town as the sun soldiers its way higher into the sky, until P.A. wants some real rest. "I know a place. Called the Goat Farm."

"Goat Farm? What's that?" I know he's got strange friends, people I've never met, but farmers?

He points west, or what I guess is west. I mash down the gas and the engine coughs. A man's standing next to an intersection, hands in his pockets, shouting at the sun. We miss the turn a couple times and have to circle back. Finally, we pull in front of a place P.A. figures is the one. "Here."

I run my eyes across the yard, the splintering shack.

P.A. cuts me off before I can ask. "Lady who owns the place used to raise goats."

"But she's got space to spare?"

"There's only one bed, Tex." His face hangs slack and blue. His future spreads out in front of me—his limbs rigid, froth between his teeth. "Sorry."

I let him out, drive off. He really was sorry. You could tell.

I pull off the highway and sleep for hours, days maybe. I dream of joining a group of drifters, big-hearted people who take me in and share what little they have, going from city to city together, each of us making sure the next is fed. When I wake up, night soaks everything. Streetlights flick nearby. A crow sits perched on the pickup's hood. It takes four tries to turn the engine over and send the bird flapping away.

Interstate traffic pumps me down to North Hollywood, and to escape, I slide into the nearly empty lot outside a McDonald's. There's a group of junkies sitting cross-legged, leaning against a dumpster. One sits up as I get nearer and I ask how he's doing. He has on ripped-up jean shorts, his legs shedding layers of skin.

"If you had to guess?" He scratches dead skin off his sideburn.

"Probably seen better days, I'd say."

"Damn."

"What?"

"What kind of awards they give you for all that genius you got between your ears?"

"Why don't y'all just go to a mission?"

"Mission's for the weak."

A sedan inches along the drive-thru. I think of the little tricks Hank taught me: how to lift an order off the counter inside a fast-food joint before someone has a chance to claim it, and how to skip the pay window altogether, act rushed and aggravated at the second so you can blast out of the lot before anyone realizes you didn't pay the bill. "You'll be hungry and alone one day," he told me.

I plop on my ass, cross my legs, the dumpster against my back. We, the junkies and I, don't speak for a while. It's the kind of quiet camaraderie I could get used to. The other two eventually sprawl out on the pavement, and I picture Hank again, his body not at all looking like he was just asleep when I found him. That was a trick, too, one that went wrong. He showed me how to crush the pill like bone into powder, to use the Bic lighter to make liquid in the bowl of the spoon.

I fade off like the others, crossing into the black with the warm sense of security that stray dogs must feel when they travel in packs. I awake to the press of cold steel against my neck. A piece of scrap metal, sharp edged and rusted. The dreamers are gone, and when I ask what's going on, the junkie with the ripped jean shorts jams part of his fist damn near all the way into my throat. "I need to go somewhere. I need to get out of this fuckin' town. You understand?"

I gag.

"Nod."

I nod. He yanks his fist from between my teeth.

"Who's stopping you?"

"Not you." He presses the mangle of steel to my neck, pats my pockets with his free hand. He finds my keys and strolls off to the pickup, climbs in. The engine sputters, then groans, and on the fourth try, the junkie gives up and drops out of the pickup, his face red.

He points a bone-thin finger at me, accusatory. "I need to get the fuck out of this town."

I keep quiet.

"You understand?" He fastballs the keys into my face, walks off. "You understand?"

Blood leaks warm from my right eye. I do understand. Really, I do.

The McDonald's lights flip off. A lady in a uniform walks out into the lot, stops when she spots me toweling blood from my face with my T-shirt, then turns the opposite way. I stand, make to leave. The pickup starts first try. A throb in my throat makes me think I might never see P.A. or Face or Minimum Wage Mama again. My mattress's still back at the townhome, but no way am I phoning the landlord. It first hits me, that I can still go home and help Ma get right, like a shiv in the neck. My foot kicks down on the gas.

The pickup screams to the freeway, but the getaway isn't

as dramatic as I hoped. Traffic clogs the lanes after a few minutes. I sit behind Mack trucks and minivans for two hours, dig in the cup holders for a cigarette butt P.A. might have left, but it's all ash. After a couple miles, I exit and skid to a stop at a 7-Eleven. I drop fifty cents in the pay phone, but the landlord doesn't answer. I try my boss at T.J.Maxx, to let him know I'm going home, but it's no use.

Morning blinks the world bright. I never look in the rearview. Los Angeles never shrivels in the rearview behind me. The traffic spreads apart like phlegm. I floor it through exhaust clouds and barrel east on I-10, a straight shot to El Paso. Slanting saguaros and Waffle House parking lots whoosh past. Flames chew away a crashed car. An eighteen-wheeler's tipped on its side. Every now and then, Hank appears in the passenger seat, but he fizzles off before I can get a word in. If I make it home, I tell myself, I'll see him clearly, the wild smile that revealed streaks of cigarette stains on his front teeth.

The junction for I-20 appears out of nowhere. I swing left just in time. I drive through the day, then through the night, honking at semis and blinking at empty fields all the way home. The Dallas skyline reaches its fingers into the sky. North Texas isn't much to look at, but if you don't keep your wits about you, it'll leave you for dead.

The tires kick up gravel in the driveway. The sun struggles up over the silhouettes of trailers and shacks lining the road. I pound the front door until my knuckles ache something awful. Ma opens, sleeves the sleep from her eyes, tugs at a knot in her hair. "You made it home, honey."

"I called." I pluck a bouquet of plastic flowers off the mantel. "I'm going out."

I don't expect her to fight me on it, but she looks like she could cry. "Already?"

Then, she thumbs her lighter, lights a smoke, lies flat-backed on the couch and lets out a little laugh. "Already?" She laughs harder. "Already, already, already."

The walk takes twenty minutes, past the middle school I attended, along the sidewalks in front of the old, abandoned homes where Hank and I used to kick in the backdoors and pound Keystone Ice. Where we used to inhale crushed-up painkillers. Where we'd talk all night about how far we'd crawl on raw knees to get out of this town.

I unlatch the cemetery gate. Gnats, a swarm of them, buzz all around me. I stomp up and down every row. People who lost someone, I guess, have leaned fresh flowers against the headstones. They must be real torn up, I know, but so what?

My footsteps echo loudly in the morning quiet. I consider life, the way it tosses you from one place to the next until you slam face first into the wall. The way some hand you can't see takes a fistful of your guts and forces you back to your feet. I make up my mind to say goodbye to Hank one last time, then tear ass back west. I picture P.A. asleep at the Goat Ranch, the fires chewing through the mountains. I imagine the landlord plastering the holes in the wall, Face and Minimum Wage Mama doing whatever they're doing, wherever they ended up.

The clouds grow gray as cadavers and sag so low they damn near touch the headstones. I search and search, but there's no telling where we buried Hank. I wind up, hurl the bouquet at a random grave. It slaps the stone. Those plastic petals look ridiculous—and I laugh, I really do—next to all those living, breathing flowers.

DEAD CATS

I'd known Coach Tarp since the first year of middle school, had seen him turn from nice to just alright to all hateful like, and I didn't appreciate the way he sized me up right now. Like he'd never seen me before in his life.

It must have been a hundred degrees outside, and we were boiling in the locker room, a little brick shack thick with the stink of sweat. It was our first day of ninth-grade football. Coach Tarp smiled at a slant and slapped a hard hand on my shoulder, nudged his assistant coach and said, This boy'll make a damn fine tackle dummy for some big bastard whose sack has already filled up, will he not?

I'm not a tackle dummy, I told him. I knew I was talking bullshit, but I also knew you were meant to protest when someone ragged on you like that. I plan to play, Coach.

Alright, alright, son, he said, and laughed. He nudged

me with the sharp of his elbow, made a face to say he was just giving me a hard time. Still, I knew he meant what he said, at least in part, and although I had protested, I couldn't have given less of a shit about football. A few kids in the locker room cut up with him. I didn't even hold it against them. Besides, they'd all end up on the B-team with me and the rest of the players whose names Coach couldn't seem to recall. I would've signed up as the water boy if that meant an extra two hours I didn't have to go home to my old man. He had a real rotten temper those days. A dirty dish forgotten in the kitchen sink and you were out front doing wind sprints, him hollering at you to stop dragging ass. Leave the lights in the living room on and you were under the hot sun in the yard pulling weeds all day. Talk while the Cowboys were on the twenty-yard line and you'd catch a backhand to the face.

The little brick shack we used for a locker room breathed hot as a motor. It was September, but most days still ran north of a hundred. Just when you'd think the weather was taking mercy on you, the next day the sun would damn near skin you alive. We suited up between the steel storage containers and laundry bins stuffed to the lip with towels. It smelled how I imagine dead cows stank. Coach Tarp sauntered back to the athletic office and lumbered around, sipping from a silver thermos that declared him COACH OF THE YEAR – 2000.

Mannard came into the locker room, chomping on chaw, chest bulging. His first name was Ricky. As long as I could recall, everyone had just called him by his dad's family name, though to my knowledge Mannard'd never known him. He was a shoo-in as starting linebacker, mean as a chainsaw. I looked up from tying my cleats and watched him hunch forward in front of the storage locker. He was sucking in heavy, slow breaths like he wanted to summon strength from somewhere deep and dark inside himself. He placed both palms flat on the locker door, steadied himself, and hammered his forehead into the steel 'til thick bolts of blood ran in zigzags down his cheeks. I looked away. How was someone meant to react to that?

Mannard was a year older than the rest of us. He'd failed ninth grade the first time around, but the school gave him another stab at it. He had mangled features and a mashed-up nose, a face like a bulldog you might find gnawing on bones beneath a busted old car in the corner of a junkyard. Acne crisscrossed his shoulders. Veins mapped his arms, thick as corndogs. Everyone had heard rumors he injected himself with testosterone from the time he was young, maybe as far back as middle school. I'd once seen him, when I was in the seventh grade, get wrestled to the earth by a kid in his class. The boy was the better brawler, that was obvious, but Mannard fought his way back to his fight and then beat him blue with a backpack full of big, thick textbooks. The campus cop came sprinting from his office, dragged Mannard away smiling a mouthful of small, gray teeth.

Mannard turned to the rest of us, grinned, slapped his bare chest twice. He swiped blood from his cheek. For the first time, I realized why I feared him. It wasn't because he was mean or scary. It was because looking at him made you feel even worse about how much you let people shit on you. Coach Tarp walked back into the locker room and folded his arms. C'mon, boys, he said, and together we all walked out to the field and lined up.

School district budgets had been slashed one year after another, and we stood on the football field among wild weeds and dying dandelions. The chalk yard lines had faded a dull white, and the goal post stood at a slant. Coach Tarp walked down the column of boys, assigning each player a position. He pointed at Mike White, a lean, muscular boy who could sprint a forty in under five seconds. You: quarterback. He pushed his finger Mannard's way: This one's easy—linebacker. He listed off each position, offensive and defensive, A-Team and B-Team, and reached me at the end of the line. You: B-Team linebacker, he said, and looked like he was trying to hide a smirk.

We on the B-Team all had to pair off across from our A-Team counterparts. We braced ourselves as they hurtled our way, ready to run right through us. When our turns came, we were meant to do our best to knock them back on their asses.

Through my facemask I could see my old man watching up in the bleachers. He held a Coke can I'd bet my kidney he'd filled with Wild Turkey. Six or seven years earlier, in Peewee League, I was half a foot taller than my teammates. I had big, bulky shoulders for my age, and could outrun anyone, even the cornerback. My old man would come to my games, a big grin always on his face. Each time I drilled someone, he would yell *goddamn right* and *that's what the fuck I'm talking about.* On weekends, we'd drive over to the YMCA weight room and he'd make me do squats 'til my knees nearly gave. But in the seventh grade, I stopped growing, my old man lost his job not long after, and he started tipping back the bottle after Ma moved out.

Mannard's turn came first. I tensed my body as best as I could. I glanced back up at my old man once more as Mannard tore ass my way. He didn't move his feet all that fast at first, but he steady built speed, nailed me like a sack of hammers. My back slammed on the ground, my breath left my lungs, and I staggered to my feet, the world soft at the edges and pocked with white specks. I stood up and got my helmet off just in time to vomit the pizza the cafeteria had served at lunch. The other players were looking at me with some kind of pity. I wished someone would laugh, but none did. The silence just made my grief all the heavier.

By the time I gathered myself, Mannard was already hunched forward across from me. I wanted to—but didn't—look up at my old man in the bleachers. I took three frantic breaths, set my legs apart in position, and then steamrolled toward him. I hit him like a battering ram but dropped like a brick. He was still standing.

Coach Tarp stood off on the sidelines with a fist knotted over his mouth. Although he tried to muffle it, he laughed from somewhere deep in his throat. What had happened in his life since he headed the weekly prayer group at our middle school, back when he nodded in sympathy as we recounted our experiences with the Lord, I couldn't say.

All practice long, the parents huddled in the bleachers. They all screamed their kids' names and clapped. My old man slouched off to the side, all on his own. He lowered his lips to his Coke can every few minutes. As I took my spot back on the B-Team side, his face was all daggers, chewed me up. I couldn't stand it and broke eye contact.

Coach Tarp turned to his assistant coach and nodded toward Mannard. Meaner than a junkyard dog, is he not? he said. That boy will be in the news every week.

I looked up again and my old man had disappeared. In an hour and a half, I would inch through the front door and find him waiting there on the couch, his hands folded over the leather belt coiled on his lap.

We were all headed to White's house, three weeks out from the first game. His family lived on N Avenue, a long line of squat, splintered shacks that sagged at awkward slants and shed paint. Bagfuls of garbage lined the street outside. His neighborhood was near mine and not much different.

It was around nine at night, a Friday, and I parked my old man's Ford Ranger far off down the street in case the cops came. They protected the other side of town, patrolled our side. Clouds welted in the sky. The only streetlights that worked flickered like bug zappers and shadows swelled and contracted. I walked up to White's and along the way passed a few men sitting on lawn chairs circled around an Igloo cooler. They spoke in quick Spanish and smashed empty beer cans under their soles.

White's parents had gone to Harrah's Casino in Shreveport, where they were probably gambling away money they didn't have. They'd made him promise not to have anyone over, but when I shouldered through the front door, there were forty or so football players shuffling around the living room. Kids slashed beer cans with pocketknives and shotgunned them right there in the kitchen. Suds splashed all over the linoleum and they cheered. On the back porch, I spotted my cousin Jack sucking on a Marlboro Red. You're limping, he pointed out.

A month of getting pounded by Mannard will do that, I told him.

Lots of tail here, he said.

Sure is, I told him. But I planned to keep my distance because I didn't know what to say if someone asked how I expected any play time this season.

Jack bucked me with his shoulder as if to say get a load of this. A few players from the A-Team were sprinting in place in the backyard. White stood off in a corner, cupping his hand over the cordless telephone and yelling into the receiver. No, there's no party here, he said, but the grunting got so loud you couldn't make sense of anything he said after that. He slid the phone into his pocket and walked over to us on the porch.

My folks just saw someone famous at the casino, but I couldn't make out his name, he said. Said he had a great big dog with him, a German shepherd.

Mannard appeared next to us. He wiped the sweat off his Keystone Light can onto his forehead. German shepherd's a good dog, he said. He tilted up the beer and drained it, crushed the can in his palm.

For as long as I could remember, Mannard had lived on my street. He stayed with his mom and stepdad, who drank on pace with my old man. Which is to say, he could put back a twelve-pack and still work on his truck 'til the sky drained of sunlight and night fell upon the neighborhood.

We had only spoken once or twice, Mannard and me. A couple summers earlier, my old man sent me outside to pick weeds, punishment for some wrongdoing I couldn't remember, maybe nothing. The sun pounded me, shredding away layers of skin on my shoulders. Ma was still around, and it seemed like every time she gave my old man hell, he sent me outside to snatch weeds. I was working fast, trying to get the whole thing over with. I stopped for a breather and saw Mannard outside on his lawn. He had a dog with him, a pit bull whose fleas you could practically see from across the street. The dog dashed alongside Mannard as he chased down stray cats. Mannard grabbed the cats by their napes and yanked them from the ground like dead flowers, stuffing them in a garbage sack.

A small, dirty cat, maybe a kitten, leaped into the hollow shell of an Oldsmobile sedan in the yard. Whatever color it was, I couldn't tell—its matted fur was tarred with oil and muck. The car had been there since before Mannard and his family ever showed up. Someone had stripped it of all its parts, and it sat propped up on cinderblocks. The side mirrors were gone, and weeds grew through the space where the engine was meant to be. I wondered how many microwave meals and six packs that Oldsmobile had paid for.

Mannard kept hunting the stray cats 'til he filled up the sack. Inside, they clawed and kicked and cried, but he just knotted it tight at the top. When his stepdad busted out of the front door, I knew Mannard was in for it. The man was thin, wiry. That meant nothing. My old man looked like he'd never eaten a lick of food in his life, but if he got his hands on you, they may as well have been steel.

Crouched in my yard, I watched his stepdad grab Mannard by the back of his neck. He jerked him down to the earth. I was old enough to know that our parents were searching for guidance as much as we were, and that when they came up short, retribution fit just fine. A breeze bustled garbage down the street, and I felt pity for Mannard. It broke your heart to learn it could happen to even him, an ass whooping.

But Mannard bounced back to his feet. He charged and drilled his stepdad, knocking him down back-first in one swift move that peeled away all my pity and let envy move into its place. Wounded, his stepdad hobbled to his feet and went inside, muttering. Mannard slung the sack over his shoulder, mounted his bike, and pedaled off, creaking like a screen door all the way down the street.

Two hours dragged past and I was still outside. I looked around at where time had rubbed patches of the yard bald, and the remaining grass felt dead and prickly under my feet. I picked weeds slower than before, distracted by what I had seen, but I also knew my old man was inside on the couch, five or six beers deep already. I heard the creaking before I saw Mannard ride up, moving as slow as a funeral.

Hey, he said.

I looked up twice before I realized he was speaking to me. Hey, I said. He was pretty worked up about the cats, huh?

What? he said, and then understood. Naw. Wasn't that. Caught me stealing smokes from his pack.

Oh, I said, and because I did not know what else to add, I asked, But where did you take those cats? Shelter or something?

Mannard laughed. Naw, he said. Not a shelter.

Where then?

Dropped them off an overpass over the highway.

I let out a laugh but stopped when I saw his face stay the same, serious.

Dropped them? You dropped them? Like onto a car?

Onto a big rig, yeah. Must have been going eighty when they hit it.

I only nodded, and he must have sensed something was wrong because he put a hand on my shoulder.

They're only dead cats, he said, squeezing. Some things are just meant for hurt.

We lost our first game, but Mannard broke the tackle record, and that was a good enough reason for everyone to celebrate. White called us all over to his house—his parents were gone again, playing blackjack in Oklahoma.

I was out back, with Jack again, and for no good reason I was wondering how everyone made it to White's, whether their parents had driven them, whether their parents had warned them to behave, whether their parents believed what everyone said, that White's folks were home chaperoning the party.

My old man had never wanted to delay his drinking, so he let me take his truck anytime I had something to do. It was a single cab, a '98, and empty cigarette cartons crackled beneath my sneakers whenever I drove it. Most of the time Jack and I drove around, each with a beer can between our legs, gassing it through red lights and laughing, looking for a parking lot where we could stand around.

In the backyard, Mannard tackled a defensive lineman, a guy maybe twice his size. Mannard ran him into a cluster of azaleas, trampled right over him. White looked at me with a resigned look on his face. They were already dead, he said, and it took me a moment to understand he meant the flowers.

Within a half hour, the place emptied. Only a few of us stood around in the kitchen, drinking the last of the canned beer. I turned away from the others and choked down one of the back pills I had lifted off my old man. I had plenty—ten, maybe eleven—but why share?

The pill hit my head. I started drinking the dregs of nearly empty beer cans left on the counter. I gave each a shake, and then winced down the piss at the bottom. Wish we had more beer, I said.

Mannard folded his arms across his chest. He had drunk eight or nine beers, but it didn't come out in the way he spoke. What we need to do, he said, all calm, is find someone to rip off.

I laughed, but then White said, I know someone. A

girl across town. She sells Xanax, four bars. Always carries a 'script on her.

Who is she? Mannard asked.

Just some girl, White said. Takes them off her headcase ma.

Wait, I said, unsure why.

We could fleece her good? Mannard asked.

I've got these airsoft guns, White explained. Look just like Uzis. We put a bit of black electric tape over the orange tip, and you can't tell the difference. Easy.

At first, I had no notion of going with them, and even thought about going home, but it was Friday—my old man would be on a warpath. Maybe it was the pills talking, but I offered to drive.

Mannard turned to me and glared hard. You sure?

Yeah, I said. Fuck it. Why not?

The pickup trembled over every bump in the road 'til we crossed the highway and the streets became smooth and easy. A country singer wailed on the radio and I twisted the knob to crank up the volume. In the passenger seat, Mannard pressed his face to the glass. His breath fogged little birthmarks on the window.

I turned into Indian Estates, a neighborhood I had only heard of. I knew kids on this side of town drove nice cars and went off to expensive schools, but all I could think was how impossible it seemed that a neighborhood like this existed in the same city as us. I almost felt guilty driving my old man's pickup—with rust on the sidewalls and his Confederate flag sticker on the back window—in an area where the pool houses were larger than any home I had ever lived in, a place where Audis and Beamers lined the curbs.

White sat in the bed of the truck, next to my old man's weed eater. He tapped on the rear window and I rolled it down. Turn here, he said. I skipped the signal and swung left.

Park here, White said. He pushed his head through the rear window and into the cab. It's around the corner.

Mannard opened the door and hopped out, and White jumped down from the bed. White told me to stay there, said he only had two masks and that we'd need to split quick.

I leaned back in my seat and listened to the country singer cry about someone he lost, a wife or a dog. My hands were shaking. I kept thinking I could plead ignorance if the law came, that I could insist I only gave them a ride across town as a favor.

But they stayed gone a long time. The pills began to fade, and as I started to feel alert again, I worried something had gone wrong. I pictured some rich parent standing at their window, phoning the police, red-and-blue lights storming up around the bend behind me.

I left the pickup running, got out, and walked down the street, following its curve, almost tiptoeing. Their bodies took shape around thirty yards out. Whatever concern I'd felt for Mannard and White washed away. Mannard had an airsoft gun trained on a girl, and White stood nearby, hustling his junk with one hand and clutching his piece with the other. The girl was digging around in her trunk, lamppost light shimmering in her blonde hair. She turned and handed what I guessed was a pill bottle to Mannard, and he pressed the piece to her forehead. She carefully crouched and lay on the curb. My heart sped up. The girl was shaking, too, and I felt fear for her. I pictured myself running full speed and hitting Mannard from behind, knocking him down just long enough for her to get away.

I took a couple breaths and prepared to push off my back foot, but Mannard and White were already sprinting my way, laughing, and plain as day it hit me that I was as guilty as anyone else. Shame shot up inside me. Then, I felt burned up with anger, anger that they'd done what they'd done, anger that I'd come along at all.

Later, when we rolled past a cop car shaded by night

in a parking lot off the road, my heart jabbed around in my chest. The interior light clicked on inside the squad car, and I looked over at Mannard for a cue. But he wasn't paying attention. He had his face in his hands, tears rolling off his fingers.

Coach Tarp told us to all sleep in the morning before the game that next Friday, but I woke before sunrise. My old man had a handful of my hair. He dragged me from my bed and slung me to my knees on the floor. A bug crawled over my foot, but when I tried to kick it off, my old man shoved me face first into my mattress. You fighting back? he said.

I said nothing, only bit down on the sheet.

Turn around, he said.

He had a Ziplock full of pills in one hand, a belt in the other. You want to tell me where you got these?

I found them, I said.

Now you're lying?

Scout's honor.

And you think it's funny, too? He tossed the pills aside and started snapping his belt, sharp.

No, sir.

He said let's see how funny it is. He belted my back raw and my heartbeat throbbed in the small of it.

I braced myself and bit down on the sheets again, but he was already done. He smacked my skull once and left the door open, humming all along the hallway the same satisfied tune he always did.

It was around ten, a few nights later, and I hadn't seen my old man since he hunted down the pills. The television was on, whispering out in the living room. I was sprawled atop the covers, sweating. My bones ached—Mannard had come to practice fired up all week. Sweat soaked my body, and I wiped a T-shirt across my chest when I stood. A knock came from my window.

I pressed my face to the glass, trying to make something sharp out of the shapes shifting about outside. It took a moment for my eyes to adjust, but Mannard was standing there. He had a bruise under his eye, a black and purple spot. I opened the window.

I wasn't about to ask, but he said, He got me good while I was asleep.

Sorry, I offered because I didn't know what else to say. I asked if he wanted to come inside.

Not why I'm here. Listen, he said. I want your help with something.

I climbed out the window and he pulled a pack of Marlboro Reds from his pocket. He lit one and passed it to me, then lit another for himself. We walked down to the street and followed it to a T-intersection, where an abandoned home was nearly blocked from sight by shoulder-high weeds. Get a load of this, he said, pressing through the brush and stopping at a bush. He pulled up a Go-Ped.

How'd you get that? I asked.

Across town. Let's go for a ride, yeah?

I climbed on behind him, steadied myself with my hands on his shoulders—they felt like railroad ties. We rode past burned-out streetlights and shadows, bounced over potholes that felt as big as craters. I never asked where we were headed, but then the homes stopped and the street shot us out onto 14th, where a small shopping strip housed a Taco Bell, the Mexican Bazaar, and the Eastside Easy Pawn Shop.

He killed the motor and said he needed to go inside.

I was looking at the Bazaar.

No, he said, pointing at the pawn shop. Here.

But I still didn't follow.

I'll be quick.

I understood and told him I was sorry but that my old man would—

Naw, man, he cut me off. You stay outside. That's all.

Just shout if someone comes. You can hide over there. He pointed at a leafless tree next to the Taco Bell.

Man, I want to help, but . . .

Just make like you're waiting for a ride. Aren't going to be any problems.

I tried to make myself small under a scatter of shadows beneath the tree. He snapped the lock on the steel gate and elbowed a break in the glass door. A tingle crawled through my arms and legs. My chest grew tight. Clouds charcoaled, snarling in the sky.

Something shattered inside the pawnshop, and after a few moments the alarm screamed across the parking lot. Mannard appeared in the doorway, waving his arms. Just go, he said.

I left him the Go-Ped and tore off. I hadn't made it a hundred yards when I looked back over my shoulder and saw the cruiser skid into the parking lot, its red-and-blue lights staining the store fronts. I ran 'til I thought I would retch, and then I ran faster, turning down a street leading to our neighborhood, the shadows lashing my body all the way home.

I stayed home from school sick with worry for two days. I really was ill, holed up in my bedroom. I chewed the tips of my thumbs raw and waited for a knock on the front door.

But no one ever came looking for me. On the third day, I went out to the living room and sat next to my old man on the sofa. The Cowboys were down by seven, and he was in a foul mood. Troy Aikman threw another interception, and my old man hurled a beer can at the screen. Worthless, he said. Fuckin' worthless.

He grabbed the clicker and flipped channels 'til he found the local news. The presenter was talking about rising youth crime in town, and her face tightened as she went on. A young robber had targeted a local pawnshop, she said, shuffling a stack of papers in front of her. She said the police department had arrested a star football player in connection with the incident.

Mannard's mugshot appeared on the screen, and I wondered how he looked so calm staring into his ruined life. My old man shot me a look and my back stiffened. Ricky Mannard had a promising future ahead of him, the presenter explained. But he made a grim choice. When the police arrived, he was fleeing the scene of the crime on a motorized scooter. He had a backpack full of cash, an old radio, and three firearms he allegedly stole.

As it turned out, the cops damn near opened fire on Mannard. He tried to outrun the cruiser but didn't make it far. He hopped off the Go-Ped and cocked a shotgun, aimed it right at the officers chasing him. But when he pointed it up to fire off a warning shot and pulled the trigger, the gun only clicked. My old man now stared at me sideways. That's the boy lives right across the street? he said.

I stayed quiet.

It is, isn't it? he said. Sweat crawled on my forehead. What a goddamn shame.

Within a week's time, Coach Tarp moved me into the starting position. He had no choice, but it felt like Mannard had given me a gift of some sort. A strange sense of hope filled me, and I started thinking I may just make it out of town one day. You'll do fine, Coach told me. Then he stared hard at me, like he wasn't so certain, and slapped me on the shoulder.

My old man even started talking to me. I would come home from practice each day, the sunset bruising the sky outside, and he would be there, sober and ready to talk about my future. He wanted me to spend more time on the squat rack. He taught me his favorite formations when he played ball in high school. He made sure I got to bed at a decent hour. He phoned a coach at a D-3 school somewhere out in East Texas.

He showed up to the first game I started. He wore a new T-shirt still stiff with starch. TEXAS FOOTBALL, it read in big block letters. He shook hands with the other parents, taking a seat next to them and resting his elbows on his knees. When I looked up right before the starting whistle, he was cutting up with the Whites. He pointed down at the football field, right at me, and I waved their way.

But I played awfully. I barreled at whoever carried the ball and wound up flat on my back, cleat marks across the chest of my jersey. I drove headfirst with closed eyes and missed my target every time. I leaped and landed on my face guard. When the bullhorns blew and half-time was called, I jogged to the bench and sat, scanning the bleachers. My old man was shaking his head, hobbling down the steps. He slipped a flask from his pocket and disappeared behind a row of trucks in the parking lot.

One night about halfway through the season, I understood I had blown it for good. It was nearly November, shortly before dusk, but it felt as if the whole world was aflame. I walked home and found my old man crumpled on the couch, beer cans piled up around his feet on the carpet. The can of Keystone Light in his hand was sweating.

At least I made the starting lineup, I said, but the words tasted false in my mouth. His head sagged low to his chest. He closed his eyes, but I kept at it. If I keep at it, I may get good enough to play ball in college. Maybe even a scholarship.

The Cowboys gathered on the thirty-yard line. The quarterback squatted into position. The others fell into a shotgun formation. My old man cracked one eye and fixed it on the screen. The quarterback ran a few yards to the left and found his footing. Together, my old man and I watched him cock his arm back and let loose. The ball arched high, shivered in an uneasy spiral—an interception. I looked back at my old man on the couch. He took a swig of beer. What a goddamn shame, he said.

Outside the dusk gathered and the air ran the coolest it had in months. I crossed the street and climbed into the Oldsmobile in Mannard's yard. The kitten was curled up in the glove box, still stained with oil. I petted the cat, but when I tried to scoop him into my arms, he scratched and contorted and wrestled himself away. I sat for a second in the driver's seat, watching the shadows outside shift and shiver. A breeze picked up. Then, I was on my feet, exhaustion spreading through my body and down into my limbs. Even as the wind knocked around in the night, I sweat in sheets. I sprinted 'til my legs burned. The cat leaped from a bush and I dove for it, snatched at its nape, but I came back empty-handed, and when I hit the hard earth, my body rolled and rolled and rolled until it stopped.

GENERAL HOLY WAR

Awake early, I waltz to the living room of our trailer home with big plans to witness bloodshed. But what I find on the old wood-framed television Ma keeps promising to replace is public programming. I'm eleven, old enough to get pissed off that Marlboro Reds lies sprawled out on the old pullout couch, snoring. I look at him, survey the rough hands braided across this chest, the knuckles fat from too much cracking. I glance back at the screen, wonder if it's safe to flip the channel.

Each morning I bust ass to the living room, sure Marlboro Reds has hit the road, always finding him there in too-big boxers and no shirt asleep and angry beneath the sleep. My old man's gone, and ever since he got gone, Ma brings home guys you couldn't pay me enough dollars to like, guys like Marlboro Reds. There's been a few, too. She opens our trailer to just about any sad bastard she meets at the bar where she works, this rundown spot where men drink Natural Light and Keystone Light and Coors Light. Ma says they all whistle at her and say, Hey, honey, how about another cold one. Ma says her customers all work the same lowlife jobs, the kind you only take if you can't get good jobs, all collect cans at the beach or wait under the sharp sun behind the Home Depot for a day-labor gig or sometimes work the front door of Ma's bar, though Ma's bar is small and never crowded and it makes no sense anyone would need to mind the door.

My old man had got hauled off to state jail about two years ago. Ma works six nights a week at the bar. When there's not a new man, I get nights to myself, can roam the trailer park and smoke Ma's snubbed-out cigarette butts and crush ladybugs beneath my sneaker soles and crawl up the pipe on the back of the house up to the roof to adjust the satellite to pick up skin flicks I watch through static until I fall asleep.

Marlboro Reds won't last because none of the men Ma brings home lasts, not long. They come, go, come back, and go again, and I don't think about them by their names because why bother. Of course, I know their names and call them sir—I know better than to not call them sir—but in my head, I think of them by whatever they smoke. They all smoke.

American Spirits, Camel Milds, and Lucky Strikes each split after a couple weeks. They called taxis and took off while Ma was at work or hitched rides off the freeway around the bend where the big trucks with eighteen wheels and the colorless Hondas blast past all day and night heading wherever they go. They take Ma's jewelry or the wads of cash she keeps in the brown box under her bed that she's told me to not ever peek in because next to the wads of cash there are condoms. They leave behind crusted socks. They leave behind skidmarked drawers. I like the times when they leave because it's just Ma and me and we are happy alone but they never stay gone for long because another one comes and they're all the same.

I fix myself a bowl of cereal from the store brand box Ma buys me for breakfast. I sit on the edge of the couch and look again at Marlboro Reds. We've had this couch my whole life. Duct tape holds together the spots where the cushions are gashed open from our bottoms always being there. Maybe Marlboro Reds has nowhere better to be. Maybe he's hiding from bad things he's done to other people. I don't care. What I care about is he's been here two months, a real long time, longer than American Spirits and longer than Camel Milds and Lucky Strikes. He thinks we've all voted him King of the Goddamn Television, what with the way he sleeps there and sits there all day and sloshes beer on the coffee table and tosses the crushed cans in a pile on the carpet.

I keep careful to not make much noise. I hardly chew the cereal, the sharp pieces scratching my throat on the way down when I swallow a mouthful. The clock says ten past nine and Road Runner is surely already hammering Wile E. Coyote's ass, dropping big bushels of Acme Bricks on the coyote and painting tunnels on mountainsides and watching the coyote burn down the highway and crash into them, a bag of bones.

Fuck it, I think, and reach for the clicker. But soon as my fingers touch it Marlboro Reds is stirring. Marlboro Reds always stirs if I reach for the clicker. He sleeps through television shows on full blast and never moves his eyelids when I shout every bad word I know or slam the front door over and over. If I change the channel, he flies to his feet like the washed-up men and sleepless vets at Ma's bar hopping from a barstool to brawl.

The smell of cigarettes soaks everything. I know enough to know you just have to stomach some letdowns. I leave on public programming. On the screen staring back at me is a fat-faced man with big bushy tufts of red hair on his cheeks, the words on the bottom of the screen *General Holy War's Battle Hour.* General Holy War is angry. He's shouting. He's saying *freedom* and *family* and *faith* and *folk*. He's clasping his hands like he's praying and saying we have to honor the Founding Fathers.

My fifth-grade teacher has told us about the Founding Fathers again and again. I'm a bad student. I spend those class periods drawing in my notebook heads chopped off and writing the worst words I know, the ones I hear at the bar when Ma takes me with her to pick up her paycheck: *jizzflap*, *asscock*, *fucktits*.

General Holy War's real worked up. The Founding Fathers want us to be happy. Marlboro Reds coughs and hammers his chest once with a fist and never wakes up. The living room window is half open, and I hear from inside the sounds of the other trailer park kids letting loose outside like they let loose every Saturday. They run in packs and hurl water balloons at one another, let them rip like hand grenades and shout fire in the hole. I have gone out there before. I had no water balloons. The other trailer park kids pounded me with balloons until my shirt soaked through and I ran off quick, ducking back into the trailer.

I imagine Marlboro Reds in the yard, maybe working on the rusty van he drives, and getting slammed with water balloons, retreating. Then, I imagine him out, maybe a wrench in hand, head under the hood, and real grenades bursting the van into metal parts. I imagine him now stumbling in the yard with big shrapnel gashes across his chest. I imagine Ma watching him take a last step and him falling face first into the balding grass yard and Ma draping a white blanket over his not-breathing body. Just you and me for a while, honey, she's saying.

General Holy War points to the letters written on his black T-shirt: GOOD GUY WITH A GUN. General Holy War says, We should be willing to die for these freedoms and it says so right here. He's thumping a pocket-sized Constitution with a fingernail, waving the booklet around. If they disarm our populace, he says, we ain't got nothing left to protect ourselves from nothing else, maybe even from a hostile foreign force coming to take our lands and liberties and homes. The time will come when you have to stand up.

I'm thinking, Yeah, yeah, and getting up and walking back to my room. Just for the shit of it, I scream *jizzflap* and *asscock* until my throat aches awful and slam the door as hard as I can once and twice, but I never can slam the door hard enough.

Summer break starts and I sit inside where the air conditioning only sputters and coughs dust, and life in the trailer park takes a turn for the worse. I start to go outside every day. The trailer park is big and has a lot of kids and some don't wear shoes and others chew dip they steal from their fathers. A group of older trailer park boys chases down every kid they feel like chasing down. They have Super Soakers and when they catch you, they yank your pants down clean to your ankles, spray you good, and maybe spit on your ass and call you *spitass.* They hop on their bicycles and peel away and around the corner they laugh.

In my bedroom, I rifle through clothes in the top drawer of my dresser. I fish out a tank top and it's black and large and belonged to my old man. It has an American flag patch and I run my fingers along its edges. It smells like my father. I slide into the shirt, walk to the mirror, flex my arms in the mirror. I have no muscles. Ma says it's because I only eat store brand cereal but there is nothing else in the cabinets and fridge. I search for something else to eat. On my arm is a small clump, scar tissue, atop my right bicep.

Ma says my father is bad, but he's not all that bad. He used to take me to her bar and sit me on the stool and after drinking his beers, he'd ask me did I want to split to a better joint and find some serious tail. I'd say, Tail?

The scar tissue is from the night my father made a mistake and sent everything sideways. He came home from the bar stumbling and red-faced and saying Ma made him pay his check for his beers. Also his whiskeys. He stomped in circles around the coffee table and went back and forth to the fridge and each time with a new beer in his hand. You aren't tough enough, he told me. He sucked on his cigarette and held the smoke in his chest until it filled and he looked like he might explode into parts of a person. Son, he said, you aren't tough enough. Come here, he said, and grabbed my arm and squeezed to keep it still and reached out with his cigarette. The tip burned hot. Steady, he said, and burned me good. Now they'll know you're tough. Now nobody's going to hurt you. When Ma came home, she said, Goddamnit I've had enough. She called 911, yelling her head off. I won't let nobody hurt you, she said, and hugged me. Through the window I watched the lights flash on the faces of trailers blue and red and the shadow of my father in the backseat leaning forward.

I need to get strong, I think. I do push-ups until I hit ten and do more until I lose count. I do push-ups until my arms can't work. I stand up again and see myself in the mirror, but I don't look any stronger. I think hard and long and can't remember what kind of cigarettes my father smoked.

Two weeks or three into summer break and I go outside and walk to the entrance of the trailer park. I pass the sign that says DON'T STAY GONE TOO LONG. The mailbox needs a key. When its door opens, it's spitting out coupon sheets and letters with stamps and bills. I pick up the envelopes from the ground, look through the coupons, and flip through what's left. There's nothing from the state jail. I turn and pass the sign that on this side says WELCOME HOME and walk back toward the trailer.

Something wet smacks the back of my neck as I turn the corner of the gravel path. Four or five boys are staring at me when I turn around, all on their bicycles. They have faces flecked with acne. They all have Super Soakers. They're smiling. I wrench and run but by the time I get away I'm damp through my shirt and shorts.

I push through the door and my shoes squish on linoleum. Marlboro Reds shoots up from the couch. He grabs my collar and twists until I cough and says, You shouldn't be tracking water in here. Yes, sir, I manage. He twists until his clenched palm faces the ceiling. Yes, sir.

Next Saturday I sit on the porch cross-legged. I pick up ants and say, Fuck you, and pinch them dead, mash them until they're nothing. I try to eat one because I saw it on TV once. It's sour and I spit and spit but the taste stays. The sun rises high in the sky and bleeds like yolk. Marlboro Reds turns the TV up inside, General Holy

War gumming about guns. The older trailer park boys pedal past on their bicycles and I make myself small, hug my knees to my chest and try to knot up.

When they're gone, I do jumping jacks in the yard until my legs burn up and then do some more. When my father was still here, the older boys would roll up near our yard and take one look at him, the bluing jailhouse tattoo on his neck, and swing a U-turn. Day after he left, after everyone came out and cracked beer cans and watched the cop car drive him away, Jimmy skidded his bike out front and told me, Your old man can't protect you no more, huh. Jimmy was the meanest of the older trailer park boys, the leader. He has red hair and lost a front tooth and wears no shirt and cutoff jean shorts with one leg longer than the other. I looked at the pimples on his chest, red from mashing, and said nothing.

When my legs go rubbery, I switch to push-ups, crank them out until my arms ache. I picture myself strong. I see myself throwing punches at anyone dumb enough to Super Soaker spray me again. Ma's Honda rounds the corner and grinds into the driveway, tossing gravel every way. It's red and rust has eaten away much of the color on its hood. I haven't let Ma drive me to school in years. The engine ticks and she steps out. She looks at the trash cans toppled at the road, my bike on its side in the grass.

Wind blows a Natural Light can past her. It wasn't me, I tell her, meaning the garbage.

Worry lines shatter her forehead, but she smiles. I squash an ant. I can clean it up, though, I tell her.

You can, huh? Ma smiles, eyeballs me. You must want something.

I don't, but I say a pellet gun.

Forget it. Not happening.

I frown, make a big show of it.

OK, I say, a Super Soaker.

A Super Squirter? That sounds expensive.

Super Soaker, I hiss, embarrassed for her. The words shoot out meaner than I want them to sound.

Work's been slow, Ma says. She frowns. Maybe later this summer. Ma goes up the steps and disappears into the trailer. I sit on the porch, cross and uncross my legs, listen to the war cries from the other trailer park kids around the bend. The clouds above break apart. The sun smears the sky.

The older boys are riding bicycles this way; I hear them kicking at their pedals and shouting words like *fuckface* and *fartdick*. A plastic bag twists in the air and then flies low and snags on weeds. I get up and go inside.

Another week passes, then two more. I'm in the front yard every day doing push-ups. I'm up from ten to twenty-five. When I lower my chest to the earth, the grass blades poke it. I start doing sitting ups and squat jumps I've seen on the television. I tie buckets filled with water to each end of the broomstick and do curls.

Ma works late. I hear her every morning when she comes home, the sun not up but purpling the sky through my bedroom window. Marlboro Reds stays up and watches TV and throws beer cans at the front door when he's finished them. Sometimes the springs from her bed start squeaking fast and I bury my head beneath my pillow until they stop. I check the mailbox every day. No letters come from the state jail.

One day halfway through summer, I eat my store-bought cereal and pass Marlboro Reds on the couch on my way out front. I do push-ups, thirty. I hold the push-up at the bottom until my arms can't hold me up. I fall face-first into the grass.

In the yard across from ours a girl appears. She's Susanne, a classmate. She wears a flower-printed dress, has a purple bow lashed to her hair. I've sat behind her or next to her since the third or fourth grade, I guess, but she's never spoken to me. I couldn't meet her eyes if I tried. Barbies are strewn across her lawn. Sunlight snaps off the aluminum foil in her windows. Her house sits on cinderblocks. Her family's not leaving anytime soon, I think, and smile.

Susanne dances across her lawn, skipping over spots champed grassless by sun. Her little sister peels part of the aluminum foil back and watches from the window. Susanne's shoulders are tanned. I think Susanne's gone to the pool, the beach. I imagine her in a swimsuit. She jumps and twists and balances on one leg. I understand I'm staring at her and a knot twists my guts. I swallow and my throat feels crowded with thorns.

I turn away. Someone's stacked a pile of old tires on the corner. I look to Ma's Honda, the scratches all across the door panels. Back over my shoulder Ma stands at the window, grinning.

Later, inside, Ma gives me grief about Susanne. How about that Summer, she says. That your girlfriend? I make my face mean. I tell Ma her name's Susanne, but she doubles down. I'm embarrassed, she says, to forget my daughter-in-law's name. Don't tell her, please. Angry, I say, OK. Nothing else. OK shuts her up and I feel bad for spoiling her fun. Ma lights a Virginia Slim and looks out the window. I go back outside.

Hammers are hammering metal somewhere far off.

Susanne's on a beach towel in her yard, but she's now changed into shorts and a T-shirt. I feel robbed. Sunlight bounces off antennas everywhere. Bicycles creak. Jimmy rounds the bend, then the others. Dust storms swirl around them. I jump to my feet and turn toward the door. I look back and see Jimmy let loose, lift his Super Soaker, spray Susanne. I pause, but then I step inside and close the door.

I look out the window and Susanne's ringing water out of her shirt. She looks up at me, the first time ever, and mouths the word *jerk*.

Next morning, I blink my bedroom into focus and see Ma above me. She's smiling big, hunched over. She's got my shoulders in her hands and is shaking. What? I say. What's the emergency?

Hon, Ma says. Her voice is rough, like it's the first time she's spoken today. Go to Wal-Mart with me? Please?

Ma, I protest.

Ma throws her hands up, says it's the only time she has, that she can't carry all the bags herself. I'm working the rest of the week, she says. Just help me out?

I think hard and can't find an excuse. I rub my eyes, nod.

We pass through the doors that open on their own into the side with groceries. Cool air hits me. Families are scrambling everywhere, plucking cans and boxes from shelves. Some bicker. There are too many conversations and I can't separate one from the next.

Ma makes her way up and down the aisles. She snatches canned food, the shitty stuff. Green beans, red beans, baked beans. She grabs store brand cereal. She grabs oatmeal. My stomach flips around inside me. Ma writes down prices in a notebook and does math, whispering to herself. Ma puts the notebook in her purse and pushes the cart away from the groceries. I worry she's heading to the clothes, but it's too early for back-to-school sales. She plows forward and doesn't slow down and moves through a crowd of shoppers. She whizzes past a rack of basketballs. I can hardly keep up. She turns down the last aisle and looks back, cuts me a small smile.

By the time I get to Ma, she's holding a Nerf Super Soaker. It has an orange pump and a matching plastic grip, a clear bottle fixed to the top for extra water. But Ma, I say, but she just drops the Super Soaker in the cart. It's been a rough few months, she says. Things are still tight. Sorry I can't get you the bigger one.

I hug my arms around her waist.

Outside, the sun beats down on the parking lot pavement. I ignore the heat. I'm careful not to complain. I lift groceries and put them in the trunk. In the passenger seat, the Super Soaker sits in my lap. I have big thoughts. I see myself with war paint on my face, maybe a bandana cinched around my forehead. I see the older boys in the trailer park tearing ass, diving for cover. I see myself giving chase, not giving them any mercy.

Next morning, I find my bicycle in the yard and pedal out. I circle the trailer park two, three times, slowing in front of Susanne's house. She never comes out. To myself I say the phrases General Holy War says on TV. It's time for a prayer meeting, he says. Face down on the floor, he says. Get ready to meet your maker.

The day burns hot. I hide behind an electrical unit, wait. A mound of trash nearby broils. The rotten food smell makes me gag, but I stay there, waiting. I clutch my Super Soaker. When the older boys in the trailer park finally ride up on their bicycles, I track them. I hunt them. I follow them until they get ready to attack younger kids, then I sprint up and spray and sprint off.

I'm a natural with a weapon. I carry a scrap of paper and keep a tally of my kills. They chase me but I run fast and cut through trailers and disappear.

When the day's too hot, I go inside to take a break. I fill a coffee mug with water at the kitchen sink, and Marlboro Reds says, Bring me a beer while you're at it, yeah? He's watching General Holy War. I hand Marlboro Reds a cold can and he grips my shoulder. I wince. Thanks, he says. You're putting on some beef, he says.

I'm trying.

That's good. I can give you some pointers one of these days.

I look at his gut sagging over his belt buckle. Yes, sir, I say.

Marlboro Reds says his father was stronger than shit. He says his father had him working out real young.

General Holy War flashes off the screen and the show ends with a blue screen. Marlboro Reds clicks the clicker and lies back and drinks the beer.

I think of my father. When I was little, he took me to the beach. We threw rocks at seagulls. If Ma was off work, she'd sit in the sand and draw with her finger, then tell us to knock it off, to not hurt the birds. Ma would bury me in the sand, but my father would laugh and flick my forehead and ask did I know about Chinese torture. I didn't.

I fill sink water into the Super Soaker and head outside. I push my bicycle past the welcome sign and the cluster of mailboxes and the laundry building. Birds huddle around puddles and drink and I send them flying when I skid the bicycle their way. Someone shouts from behind a window screen. The sun's sagging and smudging the sky orange. The moon's outline's carved into the day.

I pull back around and ride until I reach the trailer. Ma's Honda's out front. I grab the doorknob and then hear the bed squeaking. I hear grunts. I lie on the porch belly-first and do push-ups. After a while, Marlboro Reds steps out the door and looks down on me. Good boy, he says. Now do ten more.

One night a week before school starts, I sprawl on the living room floor, sunburnt and tired. The older boys don't come out as much, and I've started cutting the patrols short. The ceiling fan rattles above. The night's thick with the heat. Marlboro Reds pounds the air conditioner with a fist and it groans and quits. Goddamn, he's saying. Goddamn.

The TV's off, so I reach for the clicker. Sweating, Marlboro Reds snaps, The hell? I'm watching something.

It's off, I say. The TV's off.

I'm about to watch something.

Marlboro Reds snatches up the clicker. He gives me a look that says go away. I go outside. My Super Soaker's on the porch, but the heat's got my mind lazy and I pass it and walk to my bicycle. I push out on my bicycle. A half-moon glows above. A cluster of clouds crowd around it. I speed up, slow down, speed up, then get tired and stay slow. Cicadas whine. June bugs jump in cones of light beneath a streetlamp. Sweat sops down my sides.

Boredom sinks in like a stone in water. I turn back home, hop off my bicycle, let the metal frame tumble to the yard. On the front porch, I slip out of my tank top and flick sweat from my tummy. Through the screen door comes the sound of the bed bouncing.

I'm on my tenth push-up when a shadow shoots across the lawn so fast I wonder if it happens at all. Something snaps, a stick maybe. I wade into the yard, mosquitos circling me.

I never see the first punch coming, but then my head hurtles. My pants are down at my ankles and I'm falling, face hitting the dirt. I roll to my back, see the older boys hunched over me.

You little fuck, Jimmy's saying.

Inside, the coils hit a high screech. I wrestle myself to my hands and knees. The older boys spray me good, on my chest, my arms, my face. Jimmy fishhooks me and they spray into my mouth. It's sharp, sour. That's piss, Jimmy says. We got a new name for you. You know what it is?

Jolts of pain push through my sides and I feel fresh

scrapes on my knees. I'm coughing.

It's Piss Breath, Jimmy says. All right, Piss Breath?

The older boys make off in a flash. I'm hot with anger, but I lie there thinking how stupid I am, how reckless I'd been to get caught unarmed. Clouds charcoal the sky, disappearing the moon. The sound of their bicycles vanishes in the night, and all that's left are cicadas screaming their brains out. When they finally let up, I listen to the quiet for a long time. Finally, the front door creaks open. Ma shouts something, the TV talking behind her. Marlboro Reds appears in the doorframe, a shadowed body in underwear, scratching his gut. He says, Did you get your ass whooped? I picture him standing at a bus stop or hailing a taxi. I picture gunshot wounds and grenades. General Holy War's hitting a fever pitch. It's time, he says. Right now. It's time.

THE DUMP

James still kicks hard. Maggie hates dressing him. She begs him to make it easier on her, to stand up on his own, but he sinks into the couch. He wiggles and thrashes as she guides each of his feet into the leg of his jeans, then slides them up to his waist. A couple of times a week, a stray foot catches her in the face. There was a time when James wouldn't let anyone do anything for him. Now Maggie has to put *M*A*S*H* or whatever other TV rerun's playing on long enough to distract him.

Maggie's standing in front of the cracked bathroom mirror, makeup brush in hand. She dabs over the blue bruise James gave her earlier this morning when he booted her just beneath the left eye. She tries to tune out the noise he's making out in the living room. The trailer's walls are thin as cardboard, and she hears every sound: his coughing, his mumbling, his shouting, his knocking over the lamp. There's no real use in getting done up for what Maggie has to do—a trip to the doctor's office and a stop at the dump—but she applies foundation, snaps on her earrings, and fastens her bracelet. If her husband wants to go on playing crazy, then who says Maggie can't pretend it's still worth living until James snaps out of it and gets back their old life?

Maggie goes into the bedroom and digs between boxes in the closet. She finds her Fendi under a mound of James's old clothes. He's got a new wardrobe now—stained, old T-shirts, sweatpants with tears in the seams—and all the button-ups and slacks he used to wear have been left to clog up their only closet. She runs her finger across the Fendi's smooth leather and allows herself a smile. The repo men hauled away everything at their old home months back, but she'd hid the bag in the oven until they left.

Since James started acting like he'd lost his mind, Maggie has sat around the trailer in nighties, house slippers, and pajamas. She runs errands without makeup, wearing ripped jeans and fraying sweatshirts. Now she hooks the Fendi's strap in the crook of her arm. If James insists on going on feeling sorry for himself, putting on this whole act, she'll shoulder the weight of their responsibilities for a while longer. She strides through the living room and catches a glance of herself in the dust-coated window. She might be nearly forty, but as far as she's concerned, she still looks good.

She looks at James on the couch and sees someone who's never been honest. In all their time together, he always had a new scam. He had other identities, not invented but stolen. He once opened an online fitness supplement site and advertised off-brand vitamins as testosterone boosters. He bought and resold caffeine pills as an FDA-approved cure for the common cold. He repackaged oatmeal cookies he bought at Wal-Mart and hocked them as high-end nutrition products that reduced depression by fifty percent.

James spared no one, not even people he once loved. He'd sued his ex-wife for custody of the child he had years before he met Maggie. He never planned to win in court—he admitted he didn't want to win—but he knew his ex would lose control fighting to keep the kid, a boy named Liam. He needed to inflict punishment as much as he wanted money. Maggie had overlooked it all because he took good care of her and asked for little in return. Looking at him on the couch now, she understands he only wanted what all con artists want: to implicate you in their cons. If he ripped someone off and she got a new purse out of it, then he wasn't left lugging around all the blame on his own.

Maggie tells James to get up and opens the front door. She lets him step out first. A hot July wind whips into the trailer. James teeters and wipes his brow. "Goddamn," he says under his breath.

An improvement, Maggie thinks. For weeks he's only managed a few words a day, unhinged combinations she guesses he cooked up to convince her how bad off he really was: *assholebrain*, *fuckheadface*, *shitsnifffuck*. When he starts up, she tries to ignore him. She grabs his sleeve and helps him down the wooden steps toward the gravel driveway.

They make their way to the old Honda Accord she bought after the repo men hauled away their last car, a used Cadillac. It had been their second Cadillac. She'd scraped together enough for a down payment with what little money they had left after the eviction, when they traded the Florida coast for East Texas and moved into the half-rotted trailer on a worthless plot of land she could hardly afford the rent on.

Losing the house had been tough on both of them, but James took it especially hard. A couple months after they moved to Texas, he slipped out for a drive one night and floored the first Cadillac into a sycamore on the side of a farm road. The car ended up braided halfway up the tree and James walked away with a golf ball–sized lump on his forehead and the new need to complain about his failure to end his own life. It's a lot to hang on a car, Maggie knows, but the Honda's a reminder of just how thoroughly he wrecked their life. Back in Florida, they had lived well. Then he conned a group of retirees into investing their savings in a real estate development he never intended to build. It turned out that they were the wrong people to rip off—not the kind who come looking for you but the kind who have no reason not to tell the police.

James fumbles with the passenger side door, pounds a fist on the window, and shouts, "Fucker." Maggie comes around and opens the door for him. She reaches across the center console and sticks the key in the ignition. The radio blasts on. It's a news segment featuring a woman recounting the small army of sheriffs that came to her home to evict her and her children. Maggie clicks it off. She helps James into his seat and shuts the door.

She backs out and puts the Honda in drive, then takes her time threading through town. Before it all happened, James had driven them wherever they went. Years passed without Maggie even sitting in the driver's seat. After the Cadillac incident, she worried that she might've forgotten how to drive. But it didn't take her a long time to get the hang of it again, and she's become James's full-time driver, partly because she's too afraid to leave him at home alone.

The Honda rolls past the Piggly Wiggly and Maggie's mind drifts to last January, when everything got worse just as the cold drained the fields of green and James started disappearing for hours each day. One afternoon, Maggie was watching a talk show when the phone rang. A lady at Piggly Wiggly wanted her to know that her husband was confused and crying in the cereal aisle. On the way home James had rubbed his eyes red and swollen in the passenger seat. "I don't even remember driving there," he'd said.

"You didn't drive there." Maggie eyed her husband. She'd read that people look in a certain direction when they lie, but she couldn't remember which. "How do you think I picked you up?"

"You dropped me off, you mean?" James's face became tight.

"You walked, I guess."

James broke into tears. Maggie had to hand it to him—he still had it.

She drives past the credit union and wonders how to get money for the rent due next week. They coast past the buybuy BABY store and she wonders if James will take it so far he'll have her changing his diapers one day.

Maggie eases the Honda into the parking lot. Dr. Barnes's office sits in the middle of a cluster of storefronts. Next to it is the Barnyard Booze liquor store, across the lot a strip club called Fred's. She wonders what kind of doctor keeps an office next to a place like that, but it's the only one Medicare covers in town.

In the waiting room, Maggie and James don't speak. The air conditioning lets out a strangling sound. A TV bolted to the wall plays a daytime talk show. A woman sits in a big chair placed in front of the audience and defends her decision to leave her kids at home alone while she went out to the bar.

The woman scoffs. "The TV was on. They were fine."

Dr. Barnes appears in the doorway. He asks Maggie to come in alone. She leaves James in the waiting room, staring at the screen.

In the office, Maggie fakes a smile. "Thanks for looking over his tests, Dr. Barnes. I've been thinking about it. It must be related to the stress of everything. We lost our home and he didn't take it well."

The doctor looks up at her and raises an eyebrow in a way Maggie takes to mean friendliness. "Call me

Fred." He smiles, then thumbs through his notes and shakes his head apologetically. "Yeah, your husband's got Lewy body."

"He's got what?"

"Lewy body. A type of dementia. At least I think that's what he's got. Can't be sure until he dies, truth is."

"You can't be sure until he dies?" Maggie realizes she's chewing on the side of her thumb. "Until he's dead, dead?"

"You ever hear of a doctor slicing open someone's brain while they're still alive?"

Dr. Barnes scribbles on a prescription pad, tears a page off, and hands it to Maggie. She reads through the list.

"How long do these take to get him back to normal?"

"Normal?" A strained look passes across the doctor's face. "There's no cure. The cholinesterase inhibitor should help with memory, maybe keep him a bit more alert, but don't get your hopes up too much. Those others, they're for Parkinson's, but they ought to let him move a bit easier. He's been having some trouble, stiff muscles, I guess?"

Maggie thinks of how James carries himself now, the uneasy gait, the careful steps, and it surprises her how much research he's done to play the part right. She stuffs the prescription slip into her Fendi and stands to leave.

"Just a second now," the doctor says. "There's the issue of payment. You don't have to pay the full amount today, but it'll be six hundred and fifty before we can schedule a follow-up."

"Six fifty?" Maggie hears the panic creeping into her voice. "What about Medicare?"

"That's after the Medicare."

"How am I supposed to come up with money like that?"

"A job, I guess." The doctor pulls a pack of cigarettes from his pocket. He eyes the Fendi. "Bag like that, I bet you can scare up some money, you look hard enough. Don't got much choice, if I'm being honest. You'll need folks with more expertise than me in the future, and they don't offer the same discounts I do."

A rotten wind pitches across the dump and the summer sun smacks down. Maggie opens the trunk to get the garbage and pauses to watch James. He waddles with more effort than it ought to take. In the sunlight, she can see how much his hair's changed. He'd had a full head of peppered gray hair, but it's turned platinum white in the last two months. His legs look different, too, stubbier and weaker than she remembers. He's lost muscle and put on weight. He used to jog each morning, then do push-ups and sit-ups before breakfast, and in the evenings, they'd walk a few miles together along the coast. But she tells herself his change in appearance doesn't prove anything. She's gained a few extra pounds herself since she took over the past-due bills, the overdue tax forms, the Medicare paperwork, and welfare applications.

Carrying the first bag of trash toward the pile in the center of the dump, she thinks of her father. He'd make her prepare his dinner, wash his work clothes, pull weeds and mow the lawn, drop flowers off at her mother's gravestone. She never saw the point. It was just a box of dust down there. She turned eighteen and left the first chance she got.

Maggie drops the first bag at the base of the pile. James saunters around the edge of the dump, taking measured steps. She can't stop thinking about how much he's aged and how quickly. He's twenty-three years older than her, but she never considered their age difference that important. She decides against asking James to help with unloading the rest of the trash. She hauls another bag from the trunk toward the pile. Her bracelet snags on the plastic halfway there and liquid trails behind her on the dirt. She tosses the bag and garbage flies from it. She takes the last two bags and sets them down gently at the edge of the pile.

It occurs to her that all the junk was once part of people's lives, little fragments of who they were. She stands with her hands on her hips and catches her breath, studying the dump. There are two chairs still intact, and she pictures James and herself sitting on them while watching the sun set.

"What do you think of these chairs?" she shouts, but James doesn't reply.

She looks around and doesn't see him, worries he's found something sharp enough to cut himself with. She finds him crouched down facing the other direction at the far side of the pile, about fifteen feet off. He's leaning over something she can't see until she's close enough to get a look past his shoulder.

"Is that a cat?"

James looks back at her, then turns away again.

"James, what are you doing with that cat? It could have mange. This is a dump."

He says nothing.

"We can't take that with us."

James stands up and turns to face her. "I've had a cat before." His voice is weak. "I took good care of it."

"Well, I'm having enough trouble taking care of—"

Maggie stops herself before the words come out. She realizes that if he's faking it, what she wants to say will hurt him, and if he's not, then what's the point?

"It's a kitty." He's nearly in tears. "It'll die on its own out here."

Maggie stares at the cat. It looks a hundred years old.

"Fuckheadface," James says. "I'm going to call him Fuckheadface."

On the ride home, Maggie glances at the rearview. The cat's curled up on a grocery sack in the backseat. She drives past the Piggly Wiggly, the credit union, and the buybuy BABY store. She wonders if there's a point when someone's so past hope that you no longer owe them anything. She asks herself if there's a moment your debts to someone are wiped clean. A driver lays on the horn behind her and she realizes she's stopped at a green light. She presses down on the gas and rubs her temple with one hand, steering with the other.

"James, you really think you can take care of that cat?"

A minute or two passes. When she finally looks over at her husband, he's staring at her with his head cocked as if he has no idea what she's talking about.

At home, Maggie decides to make up her mind about whether she still believes James's faking it. She spends the afternoon reading studies online and, just in case, looks up experimental treatments and drugs that could help with dementia.

She learns that you have to catch it early and that the doctor's diagnosis would have to be wrong. She reads that Lewy body causes hallucinations, memory loss, and illogical thoughts. People with Lewy body have trouble walking, experience tremors, and lose their balance often. They sometimes drag up distant memories in sharp detail but can't recall what happened a few moments earlier. She looks up all she can find on common misdiagnoses: Vitamin deficiencies, sleep deprivation, and severe depression can cause similar symptoms, but they are all more treatable than Lewy body. She spends an hour reading about sleep apnea masks that can help, crushing up B12 tablets in meals, and googles hypothyroidism specialists, none of whom she can find within a two-hour drive.

When Maggie's eyes ache too much to look at the screen any longer, she shuts the laptop and walks to the window. James's outside with Fuckheadface. He's trying to open a can of tuna but fumbling with the can opener. Maggie goes outside and helps him. She puts the tuna in a small bowl and places it on the porch. The cat staggers over and seems to struggle to eat. She goes in and brings back a bell for James to jangle for the cat, but Fuckheadface lies down and closes his eyes.

They go inside and James sits on the couch with Fuckheadface nestled in his lap. Maggie turns on *M*A*S*H* and James nods off, sunk into the cushion with the cat twisted in a curl against him. Maggie goes back to the bedroom and takes a nap herself.

When she wakes late that afternoon, James's back on the porch. Fuckheadface's still in his lap. She watches him for a moment from the window, then goes to the phone.

Dr. Barnes picks up on the second ring. "Yeah?"

"Doctor?"

"Fred, please."

"OK, Fred."

She tells him everything she's learned. She says James can hold a normal conversation now and then. "Couldn't he just be depressed? That can mess with your memory, right?"

"Got no doubt he's depressed." Maggie hears Fred light a cigarette on the other end. "I'd be depressed if I had Lewy body."

"He doesn't know he's got that."

"I'd imagine not."

"If that's even what he's got, I mean. What I was saying—depression, sleep problems, that can cause dementia, right?"

"Chances of that being all it is are low." The doctor coughs from deep in his chest. "Real low."

"But there is a chance?"

"There's a chance I'll hire him, too. Not likely, but there's a chance."

Maggie says nothing.

The doctor coughs again, then Maggie hears him take another puff on the cigarette. "I shouldn't have said that. Sorry. Truly."

"There are these moments, Doc—Fred, when he's almost a hundred percent. He remembers stuff from before we even met."

"Again, I'm sorry, but those memories? All likelihood's they're not much more than dust in the rearview."

Maggie hasn't seen James's son more than once or twice in person, and it's been more than a decade. When he answers the phone, the voice is gruff and abrupt, not what she expected.

"What?"

"Hi, Liam." She doesn't know how to start. "This is Maggie."

Maggie only hears heavy breathing in the receiver.

"Your father's wife."

"You think I don't know who's my father's wife?"

"Right. Of course."

He doesn't say anything else, so Maggie launches into telling him everything. About James, about James's brain, about the cat. She pauses now and then to give him a chance to ask questions, but Liam only clears his throat. When she gets to the end, Maggie feels tension leave her chest.

After a while, Liam laughs a rough laugh. "Chickens, home, roosting," he says.

"I'm sorry?"

"I don't know. There's a saying like that, isn't there?"

Maggie scratches behind her ear and thinks. "I don't know anything about that."

"Look, Maggie. What I'm saying is he's never apologized to anyone for any of what he's done."

Maggie turns and looks at the window, but she can't see James from that angle. "I know you're hurt," she says, "but this is the situation. I thought you ought to know. I don't think he understands what it even means to apologize anymore."

"Why are you calling me, really?"

"I thought, I don't know, you might want to help."

"Listen." His voice is calm in a way that's more menacing than if he started yelling. "Lots of old men are shitbags. Lots of old men get sick. Most of them still have to remember the shit they did to people."

"No one deserves what he's going through," Maggie says, and for the first time, she fully believes that James could be coming apart.

"What I'm saying, Maggie, is given that he can't remember how lowdown a bastard he was, you'll just have to remember everything for—"

Maggie puts the phone in its cradle before he can finish. She fills a glass with water from the kitchen faucet and takes it outside to James. He's sitting on the lawn chair with Fuckheadface stretched out across his legs. He's petting the cat hard and rough, but it's so fast asleep it doesn't move. Maggie reaches down to rub behind the cat's ears. It takes a moment before she understands it's dead.

Maggie finds a garbage sack beneath the sink and goes outside. She scoops Fuckheadface off the porch where James left him and knots the bag, placing it at the foot of the stairs. Back inside, she sits James in front of the TV.

"I'll heat you up a Hungry-Man, but then we've got to take care of the cat."

James doesn't say anything.

She microwaves his meal, washes the dishes, and returns from the kitchen. James has a hammer and a piece of wood he's trying to nail into the window frame.

Maggie puts his dinner on the coffee table and rushes over to him, snatching the hammer.

"What are you doing?"

"Neighbors," James whispers.

"We don't have any neighbors."

"Oh, we've got neighbors, alright, and they keep poking their heads around trying to see what we're doing."

"Why don't we just sit down and eat?"

James looks at the Hungry-Man on the coffee table. "I don't want to eat that shit."

Maggie sighs and decides against fighting with him. "OK, we can eat after we put the cat to rest."

"He's not tired."

Maggie tries to explain it to James, that they need to bury Fuckheadface before he starts to smell, but James throws his arms up.

"Stop talking about this."

"Don't you want him to have a proper burial?"

"I said stop talking about it, you fuckin' asshole."

She looks in his eyes and wonders if the talk of death's upsetting him or if he can't remember the cat at all. Either way, what she sees on his face is fear.

An hour later, they're in the yard, Maggie shoveling a hole in the ground. HERE LIES FUCKHEADFACE, James writes on a makeshift crucifix, two pieces of scrap wood

Maggie nails together. They dig a small hole, and James drops the shoebox casket inside with a thud. Maggie plants the grave marker in the earth. James starts to say a prayer, but he trails off and then mumbles lyrics to an old song he used to like.

When they finish, James lies on the couch and drifts into a twitching, uneasy sleep. Maggie decides to let him rest and goes outside. On the porch, she sits and tries not to think about their old life. Loneliness sets in, a strange feeling, she thinks, when someone's always at her side. She can see her nights after this. Getting him set up on the couch. Microwavable meals. More *M*A*S*H* reruns. She imagines backing the Honda down the driveway, threading through town, and picking up speed on the highway. She lets herself picture James's son left to decide whether to help James or find him a place in a state institution. She wonders about a world where she's on her own and only responsible for herself.

Something knocks behind her. She looks back and sees James standing at the screen door. He lumbers there staring at her until she gets up and opens it for him. James stands next to her and glares out at the sunset bleeding out past the sycamores. He grabs her elbow. Softly, the way he used to. "Maggie," he says.

She studies his face and searches for some fragment of who he used to be.

"Can I ask you something?"

"You can ask me anything," she says, and feels the blood in her heart.

James looks away, then back at her, but not like before. He walks to the door and waits for her to open it for him. Before she goes in, Maggie turns and looks at the field. A turkey buzzard is feasting on the face of some dead prey. A pickup rumbles past on the road at the bottom of the driveway. Maggie pictures the doctor sinking a scalpel into James's brain, slicing away layers of meat until he finally finds certainty. She turns back toward the house and catches a glimpse of herself in the window's reflection. She watches the fog of dust the pickup left in its wake. She squints hard but can't make out whatever's behind her.

SOMETIME IN LATE '87, EARLY '88

I don't think much of it when Charley starts popping off at the mouth. He's shooting me that look, the one that says I better be game to scrap if it comes down to that. He's like that. He puffs up his chest and acts like his sack's pure steel. It doesn't matter that he's been surviving off dumpster food for so long he's practically withering away. His arms are shriveled yarn, his skin damn near see-through. Acne scars crater his face, and scabs fleck his hands and neck.

The smell of seared garbage rides the wind our way. A handful of old panhandlers, a half block down, huddle around a dumpster they've lit on fire. They're cutting up and talking shit, having fun. I'd join them, but the air's damp and the blaze won't last long. Plus, Charley snagged us a couple tall boys from a corner store, and I'd have to share. Cars hiss past now and then. Otherwise, the streets are empty tonight in Deep Ellum.

Then, I see what Charley's all worked up about: a dozen skinheads marching in columns of four from the other direction, pushing through a sheet of fog. Neon lights flash pink and purple on the pavement. I've spent my entire life in Dallas. I once saw, when my old man dragged me downtown on an errand, Klansmen swaddled in white robes. A bunch of sad fuckers holding placards, their voices too weak from cigarettes to even chant. You could see it on them, that they were scared of everything. But these skinheads are something else. They're about sixteen, seventeen, a few years younger than us, and they don't look scared at all. They're all suited up: shaved skulls and combat boots, leather jackets and patches all over.

"You ready?" Charley asks.

"Those assholes?" I say, and even I can hear the bullshit in my voice. "They couldn't land a hit on me if they had five fists each."

Charley balls his fists and spits a thick glob. I don't tell Charley, but truth is, I've never been in a fight. Or I've been in plenty of fights, but I've never won one. Even when my old man used to tee off on me, I'd just go limp and grit it out. One of the skinheads in the front column has a switchblade. He's shifting it back and forth between his hands. I swig what's left of my Natural Light, all piss, and toss the can over my shoulder. It hits the sidewalk with a clank.

The skinheads stop in front of us, and one of them gives me a quick nod. I can't tell whether he means it as a threat or a greeting, but then he spits on the ground and says, "You got a problem?" He gets chest-to-chest with me. I can smell a good home on him. The kind of place with three meals a day. Still, his face is all soaked with anger. He's got wildfires in his eyes. Charley pops off at the mouth all the time, but I can't imagine us actually getting into a brawl. When you live rough, the right kind of shit talk can get you out of most fights before they start.

I glance over at Charley. I don't know what I want from him, maybe guidance, but he's hitting me with his other look—the one he used to give me when we first started pocketing wallets and purses in bars, the one that says I better man up. He's sucking his lips in tight so his mouth can hardly hold his teeth. I don't want to let him down, but my knees are puddles.

"No," I tell the skinhead. "No problem."

"I'm asking because it looks like you've got a problem," he says.

The streetlamp glow gleams off his skull. He bumps his chest against mine, pushes me back a couple steps.

I stare down in an oil puddle, keep my face straight. I know enough to know you're supposed to come off as neither prey nor threat. I shift my weight and hear my hip pop.

"Nah," I say. "We're cool. Really."

But a riot's working its way through the skinhead. I see the way he's coaching himself to attack. A man across the street inches past, his dog on a leash, then stops next to a pay phone, digs around in his pocket, and watches us.

The panhandlers down the street laugh again. They move away from the dumpster, the fire in it dead now. They walk our way, hugging themselves against the wind and talking to each other. As they get closer, I see they're not so old; they've just been outside a long, long time. They're all layered in coats. One passes his forty. Another jangles the change in his pocket.

The skinheads whip around toward the panhandlers. The one in front of me shouts, "Get those motherfuckers." They tear off in a full sprint. Whatever the others scream, it's hard to make out. The panhandlers scatter. A couple skinheads chase one down an alley, others up the street. The skinheads catch one panhandler by his coat collar, topple him to the ground. Boots thud off the poor bastard's sides, and he balls up and wraps his arms over his head.

Charley bounces on his toes like he's about to sprint over there, but my legs are sandbags. I look up the street and see the man with his dog slam the pay phone into its cradle, hard, then walk the other way in a hurry. Charley nudges me and says, "Let's get a piece." But before he breaks away, red-and-blue lights come flashing up. A siren bawls.

A cop and his partner, both in plain clothes, bust out of the car, and the skinheads disappear down the alley. When I look back over at him, Charley's standing casually, his thumbs in his belt loops—it's his innocent bystander act, the one he does anytime cops come around. The police officers give up and reappear at the mouth of the alley. One's short, fiddling with his radio, and looks like he's been stuffed in a trash compactor. His partner's tall, more bones than meat, with a mustache he keeps tugging at. The panhandler's on the curb, blood drooling from his mouth.

"How about him?" the short one says, nodding toward the panhandler. "He want to give a statement?"

His partner laughs, lights a cigarette, and spits a wad onto the pavement.

A few minutes later, the cop car pulls off. Charley tells me, "You need to nut up—that could be you next time." He walks across the street and crouches in front of the panhandler, places his hand on his shoulder. It's almost fatherly, the way Charley consoles him, and the man mumbles through broken teeth.

Charley's right, I know it. I try to picture myself throwing fists, but it feels too dumb. The wind picks up and hits me like a chisel. I feel so weak, a raindrop could drown me. Neon lights snap off the street puddles.

It's sometime in late '87, maybe early '88. We don't keep track of dates, anyhow. The days just slime through our fingers. We eat whatever restaurants toss out. We slip into bars and sneak drinks off tables. When we split up at night, Charley disappears on his own. I sleep in my sedan, a '61 Buick, the only thing I still have from my old life.

That life ended when I left home last year. I'd thought about it forever, but it didn't happen until my mom up and left. I'd just turned eighteen and graduation was only a couple months away. "I'll be back to see you walk across that stage," she told me, and apologized but explained that my old man had made life hell. She'd be at her sister's house in Austin if I needed her. Backing down the driveway, she leaned her head out the window and blew a kiss. "I'll write," she shouted, but no letters came. When I finally phoned my aunt, she said she had no idea what the hell I was talking about—my mom hadn't called her in over a year.

A couple weeks later, my dad lost his job. He spent the days on his La-Z-Boy, a ragged old recliner that wouldn't recline because he had nailed it back together after it collapsed. One night, I was sitting on the couch while he flipped through channels. He stopped on *The Golden Girls*. Dorothy had this friend staying with her, a woman who'd just buried the person she loved. "Just like me," my old man said. "I lost your mother, and that's about what she is to me—dead."

I sat there boiling—with him, with my mom. Later, it came out that Dorothy's friend's dead lover was a woman. "That just like you, too?" I said, but he was already huffing down the hallway. He banged around in the closet and appeared in front of me a few moments later. He hurled a hammer through the TV screen and shouted, "Abnormality." He whacked me good, once on the jaw, and fell back into the La-Z-Boy.

I gathered what I could and took off. My nineteenth birthday came and went, and I was still sleeping in my Buick. I'd coast around Deep Ellum when I had enough gas. Ten years earlier, my mom would take me down here, point at every boarded-up building that used to be a bar or a bookstore. But the neighborhood's different now. Every old warehouse is a venue, every abandoned shop a bar again. Kids meet up in parking lots outside shows, smash beer bottles, choke down cigarettes.

Rust had put holes in the Buick's hood, and you could reach right through it and touch the engine. Donuts sat where the back tires had once been. The nights got cold when winter came but heat off the motor always kept me alive until morning. A couple months after I left, I drove to the old house to get a look from the outside. I don't know what I was hoping for, but I didn't expect to find that the joke was on my old man. There was an eviction notice plastered to the front door. The banks were repossessing homes all over town, pulling people out, picking their places apart piece by piece. Repo men lugged off televisions, kids cried all the way to the curb. Curling up in the backseat, I'd dream of the eviction crew yanking him right off his La-Z-Boy and tossing him out on his ass, maybe busting his nose when he lipped off. It was a happy dream, but I still woke up each time with my throat aflame.

Things changed when skinheads started storming the streets. They'd walk down the block clutching baseball bats, run off anyone sleeping outside. If they caught you, they'd throw a boot party—when they stomped you into slop. Rumors spread. It's safe to sleep here, you'd get mobbed there. This parking lot's good, that one's a death wish.

Then, I met Charley a few months back. He grew up out east in Terrell, in a shack he swears his dead mother haunts. He told me stories about life before he left home. He was real country, used to go hunting with his old man, play football with his friends, hogtie stray animals. Until someone dragged him down to Deep Ellum one night nearly two years back, he'd never left his county. He went home shithammered that night. The next day, his old man called him a disgrace, changed the locks, and shoved him out the front door.

We got along alright right from the start. Charley taught me how to lift a purse, what bakeries tossed out their food at closing time, which spigots were safe to drink from. It felt less shameful to dig around in a dumpster when you had someone next to you, gnawing on an old apple core unearthed from beneath a discarded diaper. One night, he explained his worldview. There were two types of people, he said: "The kind who swallow whatever shit gets shoved down their throats, and the kind who fight back." He wore a slick leather jacket he'd snatched off the back of a barstool.

"What kind are you?" Charley asked. I thought hard for a while but didn't have an answer.

Charley and I split up each night and I have no idea where he goes. Then, in January, maybe February, he moves into my car. He's shucked so much weight the leather jacket's like a cloak on him, and he uses it as a blanket.

"You ever see on TV, in foreign countries, when they take a big cane and crack it across someone's back?" Charley asks me one night. We're parked in a Wal-Mart parking lot, the wind rattling the Buick. "You think you could handle that?"

I think of my old man putting the hammer through the TV screen, knocking me in the jaw, but all I say is, "No. I don't think I could."

"I could. For damn sure. My dad shocked me with a cattle prod once." He slides up his shirt, shows me the stripe of scars across his stomach. "Cattle prod trumps a cane every time."

We sit quietly for a while. The engine hums. Then, Charley starts singing. Simple shit. Townes Van Zandt. Roy Orbison. Waylon Jennings. The same stuff my mom used to listen to when she holed up in her bedroom. Charley pauses now and then to take a slug from his flask. He passes it my way, and the whiskey smolders in my gut. His voice isn't much, raw and raspy, but something about the way he sings brings tears to my eyes. Real tears. I click the seat back a couple notches and close my eyes. He stops and asks what I think.

I'm all choked up, like I'm looking around inside his scarred heart. "Beautiful, man," I manage. He scrapes a scab off his forearm, squeezes out a pinch of blood. "Just beautiful."

We find a spot and sit cross-legged with our backs against the wall of a club called Honest Place. Once in a while someone tosses a coin in one of our cups, but no one says anything. They hardly look at us at all.

The club owner wanders outside, then back inside, then back outside. He smokes cigarillos and paces in tight circles. He's called Jerry, a big, rough guy who makes me nervous. You get the feeling no one's ever wronged him and got off easy. I've seen him kick people out of the club for acting up, and he doesn't call security—he takes a handful of their collars and drags them out himself. I like him alright because he never runs us off, but you can't help but hate someone who makes you realize how much of the world's shit you stomach.

When the sky drains of sunlight, nighttime falls like a blanket dropped on top of us. Crows caw from electrical lines. Cockroaches crawl past on the pavement. Charley counts his change, smiles. "Enough to get a couple beers and some bread," he says. We're meant to split everything fifty-fifty, but I slip a few coins into my pocket.

The streetlights flick on and a van skids to a stop outside the club. "Must be the band," Charley says. "You know who they got playing tonight?" I'm still trying to remember if I overheard who's scheduled when a group of skinheads spills out.

They're on us quick. I catch a knee to the skull. A fist to the chest. A boot to the ribs. When I scramble to my feet, a skinhead's already got Charley by his collar. He's cranking hard, swinging Charley so fierce they both almost fall. The next blow knocks me face-first onto the pavement.

Jerry slams through the entrance, a shotgun slung over his shoulder. "I warned you motherfuckers," he shouts. He cocks the shotgun and the skinheads scatter. Cars blast past. An ambulance screams down the street and doesn't stop. Across the street, a junkie sits up from where he's sleeping and watches. He smiles like he's just glad it's not him. I can't blame him for that. When Jerry fires off a slug, it hits a wiry skinhead in the arm. You wouldn't believe how much blood an arm's got in it.

It takes the cops an hour to show. The skinheads are long gone. Jerry gives a statement. Charley and I sit far away from one another on the curb, waiting to give ours.

"Self-defense," Jerry says. He throws his arms up at whatever the cop asks him. "Feared for my life."

Another cop walks over to us, and I recognize him from the first night we saw the skinheads mob the panhandlers. He sizes me up, tugs on his mustache a couple times, then pulls out his notepad. "What we got?" he asks. "How'd it go down?"

I look over at Charley. His mouth's open and I see he's missing a tooth. "You're asking me?" I tell the cop. Blood drips into my right eye. "I'm just a bystander. I didn't see anything."

A month passes. We get bored and spend evenings cruising around town until the gas tank runs dry. We talk about getting jobs, maybe an apartment, but we never apply anywhere. We split up during the day to cover more ground, to hit more dumpsters and bars. But Charley's haul thins out. He says people don't carry as much cash as they used to. He starts taking off for hours at night. When he comes back, his eyelids are heavy and he's too tired to help me push the Buick to another parking spot where it won't get towed.

The fourth or fifth time he shows up at the passenger-side window, slurring so hard I can hardly follow, I snap at him. "What the fuck, man? Are you holding out or something?"

"Holding out?" he says, like he's got no idea what I mean.

"Holding out," I say. "Don't be an asshole."

Charley reaches into his coat pocket, pulls out a syringe and a small baggy with a brown nugget, a crusty old spoon and a lighter. He holds it all spread out across both palms like a gift he's traveled miles to deliver.

"Hand it over."

"You sure about that?"

"Do I sound unsure?" I ask, though I can hear a shadow of hesitation in my voice.

Charley takes his time removing his belt, strapping it around the crook of my arm. When he's ready, I look away and he jabs it in a vein that's bulging like a sausage. There's a pinch, and I can't get comfortable. I fidget in the driver's seat. The heat off the engine passes over me like a wave. The junk hits my head and I let my face fall against the window. On the sidewalk, an old man staggers through a light drizzle. My breath makes maps on the glass.

"You're good," Charley says. He wipes the wound with a napkin he's found on the floorboard.

The old man's face is severe, deep lines all over his

forehead. He looks like something left outside to rot. "That guy looks like my dad," I say. "Right, Chuck?"

"How the fuck should I know?"

"Doesn't he?"

"I've never seen your dad."

"Sure you have."

"You'll be alright, buddy," he says.

"How'd you stand it? The cattle prod?"

A stillness plummets inside me like an anchor. The rain picks up, pelts the window. Charley squeezes my shoulder, digs his thumb into the meat. "You're on a good one now, is all," he says. I hardly notice when he starts rifling through my pockets. "Just lay back and listen to the angels piss."

"It's no crowbar," Charley says, winding up with the tire iron, "but it'll get the job done alright."

On the tenth, eleventh try, the padlock snaps. Charley's soaked in sweat, shivering—I can't tell if he's just cold or if it's because we haven't tied off since morning. I carry a burlap sack Charley lifted from the bed of a construction pickup earlier. Dumpsters can't give us the kind of stuff to trade for what we need, and we've already hit homes all around my old neighborhood.

Inside, someone forgot to turn off the radiators. The

heat stops us like a wall, and we both stand there looking around the living room. When my eyes adjust and I see the La-Z-Boy sitting in the corner, sadness crashes against me like a hammer. I take a piss on the chair, but I don't feel any better. Charley laughs as I zip up.

"This is where you grew up?" Charley says, shocked by its size. I ignore him. It's a nice house, sure, but it never felt like mine. He says, "This is a pretty swank place."

I dump everything in the sack onto the floor. Charley grabs a can of black beans and cuts it open with his pocketknife. He dumps half the can into his mouth and says through a mouthful of beans, "Protein." When he swallows it all down, he empties his pockets—a gold ring and a couple necklaces, a silver bracelet and a few pairs of earrings.

"Not too bad," I say. I guess we can trade it for enough junk to last half a week.

"This place is a hell of a lot bigger than our trailer," he says.

"I thought you grew up in a shack."

"Same shit."

"It's a good house," I say, though I don't know what makes a house good, and admitting that fact doesn't feel right. "But it got different when my mom left."

"Houses don't change."

"People do."

Charley's eyes wander and he loses interest. He walks off, wanders the hallway with a lighter to guide him. He lowers the flame to a spot on the wall that's gashed open. "Probably got y'all for copper wire," he guesses.

"Probably. Who gives a shit?" Truth is, I feel robbed.

Charley pulls the tire iron from his waistband and points it at the wall. "He must've cared about you some."

"How you figure?"

"He took all the family photos when he left."

"Anyone could've taken those."

"What would copper wire thieves want with photos of you and your folks?"

I don't tell Charley my old man pulled down the photos—three or four, maybe, because we never took many—the night he came home to learn my mom had left. I don't tell Charley my old man stomped the frames to shards on the living room rug, then rolled it up and walked it down to the trash can on the curb. I tell him, "Yeah, maybe you're right."

I walk to the window, look outside. Wind shakes the willow tree. Shadows quiver on the lawn. The bank's got an auction sign planted in the yard. I wonder how much the house's going for, but it doesn't matter—money that big doesn't really exist, not to me.

"Don't you have any good memories?" Charley asks.

It's a stupid question, but I consider it for a moment. "Sure. I just don't remember any of them."

"Shit, I get that. Me neither."

I get a strange feeling of guilt, like my old man's lurking somewhere nearby, spying on us as we survey the guts of his old house.

"Best memory I've got," Charley says, "is these scars."

"Doesn't much sound like a good memory."

"Well, it is. Because fuck him." I try to imagine a cattle prod pressed against my skin, searing the flesh, but Charley raises his shirt and says, "He whipped my ass good with a vacuum cord. Reminds me what kind of hurt I can take."

I think for a long moment, gnawing on something working its way around in my head. "Those scars," I ask, "are from a cord?"

"Damn near fainted after the few first minutes," he says, pride all about his face. He twists the stiffness out of his back, walks toward the front door.

I gather up everything and stuff it back into the burlap sack. It's a good haul: along with the jewelry, we've got a gold lighter, a power drill, and a signed baseball, though I can't make out whose name's on it. We step out into the cold and walk down the street toward my car.

"How much you think we can get for that shit?" Charley asks.

"I don't know. Not enough."

"Not a bad take, though." He drapes an arm over my shoulder and pulls me in, but I shuck him off. "But yeah, you're right. Not nearly enough."

Charley's different, or I am. Either way, I don't trust him. When he invites Earl to sleep in the backseat one night a few weeks later, it annoys me that he doesn't ask. Still, it's nice to be around someone who hasn't gotten under my skin yet.

Earl's an old guy, some kind of veteran. He looks like he's had shit luck. His hair's thinning and gray, and his pants always look damp. He's nice enough when he's got his wits, but if he drinks too much Olde English, he forgets how to speak and only communicates in grunts. Whatever he remembers steals his words, I guess.

One morning, Earl says, "I'm glad y'all took me in."

Y'all? I think, but I don't argue.

"Those skinheads been following me around," Earl says. "I seen them hurt some folks real bad. Good folks. Y'all seen them?"

"Yeah," Charley says. "Assholes. I'll catch one on his own when I get the chance."

I think about Charley's scars, what other bullshit he's cooked up. After a while, we prepare. Charley pulls off his belt and we tie off. When the junk sinks in, we all get quiet and float around in our own heads. I see my old man in my mind, watching me through windows, ducking behind parked cars, lurking around corners. But each time I snap out of it and focus my eyes, he disappears.

I nod off and wake up later that night, still cloudy and low. The junk's worn off, and Earl's rustling around in the backseat, too loud for me to sleep. Mist is spread across the windshield. A group of skinheads walk past, but they never see us. I swipe sleep from my eyes and turn around.

"What're you doing, Earl?" I ask, but then I see he's rubbing one out, staring right at me. I look away and a big, loose laugh knocks around in Earl's chest. "What the fuck, man?" By the time I look back, he's left a load on the floorboard.

I reach over and crank Charley's collar, twist it until he's awake and sits up. "What?" he shouts. "What's the problem? I'm trying to sleep."

"Am I fuckin' blind? I know you're sleeping."

"If you know it, then why the fuck are you waking me up?"

"That."

"'That' what?" Charley glares at me like he'd just as soon peel away my skin, but then Earl grunts and laughs again. He swivels in his seat to see. "Oh, shit." He pauses. "Well, I mean. What did you expect?"

"I didn't expect the motherfucker to blow a load all over the backseat. Make him clean that shit."

"Earl, you gotta clean that up," Charley says.

"Eat my dick," Earl says. He opens the back door and slides out.

Charley and I sit there, quiet. After a while, he says, "What now?"

"'What now' is you clean that shit."

"Listen, I'm sorry," he says, but it isn't an apology I want. It's my hands on his throat, to hurt him more than whatever bullshit he's made up about his old man ever could. "I can fix this."

"Just fuckin' clean it up," I say. Charley only sits there, scratching his arms. I turn off the engine and listen to it tick. He finally opens the door and steps out into the night. When he's gone from sight, I'm still sitting there.

March and April come, and the world warms up. The parks turn green. Then summer hits and sun burns all the grass dead. The nights get humid. All up and down

Commerce Street, the buildings sweat. When the cops show up every few days to run off panhandlers, they baton us until we clear off the sidewalks.

I land a job bussing tables at a pizzeria. I wear long sleeves to hide the marks on my arms. I steal a wristwatch to make sure I'm on time. I sometimes imagine I see Charley—at bus stops, on corners, in the bathrooms of clubs—but we still haven't crossed paths. I'm glad to not run into him. Maybe I overreacted, and I'd hide from anyone I felt I owed an apology. I make new friends, the same kind of people we used to take wallets and drinks off at the bars. I sometimes even manage to talk someone into letting me crash on their couch. But saving up for my own place isn't easy, and the dealers keep raising the price of junk.

Around eleven, one night in July, I clock out at the pizza shop and set off for my car. I walk down Commerce and try to find the moon in the sky, but clouds are crowded everywhere. I slow my pace when I reach Honest Place. Jerry's lumbering around on the sidewalk, smiling and slapping people on the shoulder. I want to ask him whatever happened after he shot the kid, but I figure it's not worth the time.

Coke cans and cellophane wrappers are all over the floorboard of my car, crumpled shirts and pants on the backseat. I dig around until I find a five-dollar bill, then head back out.

I'm looking for a place to cop when two police officers start following me. Voices speak ragged through their radios. I turn down one street, then another, lose them, and then dip into an alley to wait.

When I turn back and look farther down the alley, I see them: six, seven skinheads all circled around a pile of blankets and clothes on the ground. A skinhead brings his boot down hard and whoever's under the pile coughs. "Fuck it," another says, and they turn toward the street.

His arms look meatier and his head's shaved, but the missing tooth gives Charley away. He looks me up and down and scratches his skull. The first punch puts me on my back. I see the old panhandler crawling down the alley. Boots pound my flanks. An elbow knocks something loose in my jaw. "Fuckin' junkie," Charley shouts.

Sirens sound somewhere nearby, and the skinheads run. Only luck leads me to Charley's leg in time. I latch on and topple him as he lunges to leave. I wrap myself around him. "Wait the fuck up," he says, but they're already gone.

I squeeze Charley tight. He wrestles his switchblade from his pocket, tries to slice the arm I've cranked around his throat. If it breaks skin, I don't feel it. I tear the armband off his sleeve and punch his temple over and over until he drops the blade. I get up, pick up the knife, let him loose.

I stand there heaving, watching the old panhandler at the far end of the alley. The panhandler turns the corner and disappears. I'm halfway to my car when the shakes start up. I hunt for the bill in my pocket, but it's gone. I spot a couple skinheads leaning against a lamppost across from the old bookstore. I see my old man with the hammer in his hand. I remember what Charley asked me, what kind of person I am, and I nod their way. My muscles grab. A fresh film of sweat trembles me. My stomach spins. I know this won't end well, but I'm off the curb, taking a step into the street, then another, until the skinheads stiffen their backs. Clouds above crash into each other like fists. Neon lights flash in a puddle. In my pocket, my fingers shiver against the steel blade.

THAT FIRE'S THE WHOLE WORLD

I know the drill same as everyone else: stand up there, sob your face red and raw, let everyone tell you how brave you are. It's all bullshit, sure, but just about all the kids are sitting here in Jimmy Dodge's living room. Each Wednesday, Jimmy's parents open their home to the rest of us. The prayer group's called Athletes for Christ, and even though it was started for kids on the basketball and football teams, not everyone plays a sport. I sit here watching my classmates contort their faces in ways that make no sense. They break down in tears. Press hands to their chests. Howl confessions through snivels.

I'd stay home if I could, but Ma and I have an unspoken agreement: If I come here once a week, she doesn't ask about the cigarettes that go missing. Truth is, the pills and wine keep Ma pretty fogged. She might have no idea about this agreement.

It's late April, and the days stretch longer. Even though a heatwave hit early this year, the Dodges haven't started using their air conditioning. The blinds split sunlight across the carpet. I'm sitting cross-legged in the back behind half a dozen rows of kids I've known since kindergarten. Some of the kids come straight from practice, and everyone's sweaty. The air reeks of crusty socks, jockstraps, locker rooms.

Mrs. Dodge treads gently up and down the rows. She pours Coke into little plastic cups the other kids hold out, hands out cookies wrapped in Kleenex. Jimmy's parents are always doing little acts of kindness, but it's only because they think it will get them easy entry into heaven. As if feeding us near-expired Chips Ahoy! will get you a seat next to Jesus at the next Last Supper. Besides, Jimmy's a dickhead, and I can't imagine how they could make up for that fact. I pluck threads off their carpet, say no thanks when Mrs. Dodge reaches me. But I take the cookies when she insists—it's not like Ma's putting anything in the oven nowadays. It's not like we even have an oven, not one that works.

Coach Tarp is our youth minister, or at least that's what he calls himself. I don't know what kind of training you have to undergo to call yourself a minister, but whatever it is, I don't imagine he's done it. He's pacing back and forth up front, the same pre-sermon ritual he performs each week. He's a nervous guy, mean if you snap back at him. Sweat soaks through his shirt. He cracks his knuckles, wrenches his neck 'til it pops. All the other kids give him hell, but he brings it on himself. I just keep my distance. A couple years back, when we were gearing up for eighth-grade finals, his wife up and died. Ever since, his sermons have been different, darker. He'd been all love the sinner not the sin, but now you get the feeling he can't wait for a blaze to eat away whatever's left of the world. Maybe he just wants to be dead with his dead wife. Maybe he just wants us to be dead.

He delivers his speech—repent for this, beg mercy for that. Coach Tarp stops pacing now. The side conversations all meld together into a single buzz. He swipes the sweat off his brow. He clears his throat once, then again, and the room falls quiet. He says we're all sinners. He yells about the rapture. He warns of hellfire. "Eternity," he shouts, his voice hoarse with anger. "Y'all know how long that is?"

Some of the kids volunteer to share their stories. They put on a big show. They gripe about all the struggles they've faced in life, brag that their souls thrashed in the undertow of sin until the Lord wedged his way into their hearts. Then, they bawl their brains out. I don't know why no one can just be normal. We all have to swallow the dollar-menu slab of shit the world serves up.

I never volunteer to share my piece. My parents never went to church, anyway, and I didn't get why Ma all of a sudden wanted me to find Jesus when my old man passed. It's not like he believed—he said it was all a crock. I handle myself just fine. When I was little, I couldn't hold back the waterworks. I broke down all the time. When a gameshow contestant on the TV spoiled their shot at cashing in. If I saw a stray dog with ribs sticking out. Whenever the good guy got gunned down in a western. We break for the night around eight o'clock. I start out through the better neighborhoods in town, pass houses with flowers out front, head toward home. Nighttime falls like someone diving off a rooftop. I think about Coach Tarp screaming, the other kids crying their faces swollen. I try to remember the last time I cried. It's no use. I spark one of Ma's cigarettes, turn down the unpaved road that unravels toward the trailer park.

Saturday comes and Ma sends me to Piggly Wiggly to fetch smokes. She's worked out an agreement with the cashier. He knows what kind of shape she's in, and he's the only one who will sell to me.

The walk there, the sun's a mallet. I pass through the

automatic door and cold air nearly knocks me on my ass. Mothers toss canned vegetables and cereal boxes into their buggies. Small children chase behind them. Our cashier's on shift. He's around thirty, thirty-one, a face like someone who's always wanted to skip town but can't make it happen. He nods at me. "Your mom hanging in there?"

I can usually do the small talk, but the pity on his face today is too much. "She's doing real good, actually." At the moment, she's on the couch watching a *Jeopardy* rerun for the third time since she woke up, slugging cabernet straight from the bottle, and chewing her depression pills like hard candy. "She took up gardening. Does yoga a couple times a week."

He smiles with such kindness I almost feel for him. "Glad to hear that."

"In fact, she's planning to go back to school. Wants to study chemistry. She's training for an ultra-marathon. Also recently started painting, even sold a piece for a couple million to some gallery in New York."

The cashier's face drains. He fixes a hard stare on me. I worry for a second he might reach out and take hold of my collar. After a minute, he says, "Fuck off, kid," then shoves the Marlboros across the counter along with the change from a twenty.

I wad the bills, stuff them into my shirt pocket. I don't

tell him thanks or bye. At the automatic doors, I glance back over my shoulder. He's got this look, all wounded. Outside a car alarm blares in the lot. Crows stab their beaks at one another, fight over a piece of bread on the pavement. I send them scattering either way with a stomp of my heel. I tear the cellophane apart, cut through a pair of pickups. Head down, I nearly slam right into Coach Tarp as he slinks out of his Buick. It's a piece of shit, a beat-up old sedan with rust wrapped around the wheel wells.

"Watch out, kid."

"Sorry, Coach."

He looks down at the Marlboros in my hand.

"They're for my mom." It's technically true, so I make my face honest as possible.

"She ask you to open them too?"

I want to stay respectful, get out of here quick as possible, but it just comes out: "She recently lost all her fingers in a freak yachting accident."

"Maybe I ought to phone her up. She might want to know how you speak to adults."

"No, sir. I'm sorry."

Shame burns hot behind my cheeks. I make to leave, but he grabs my shoulder, sinks fingers into the flesh.

"Wait. You takin' care of her alright?"

"She doesn't make it easy, sir."

"Thing like that's not easy." He presses down the point of his thumb. A grown man hasn't touched me since my old man passed. A clod catches in my throat. He lets loose, pats me on the back. "Be good to her, son."

I take off across the lot, a pinch in my heart. I palm the pack until a cigarette pops and then check over my shoulder. Coach Tarp's gone. I flick a match, suck in a lungful until the smoke bites inside my chest. Fuck him, I think. I'm glad the others give him shit. Like he knows anything about Ma and me. People say he's had it rough since cancer killed his wife, even quit coaching for a couple years, slept in his sedan for a while. It's probably just talk, but I don't know why he's got to take it out on us. Everyone's got someone dead in their past.

Everything went to shit after I found my old man. Ma started watching Maury Povich and Oprah. She thought she'd become some kind grief counselor. Every day, she asked whether I'd processed my feelings. She even said it like that. "Have you let yourself process your feelings?"

I'd shoot back, do my best stab at her voice, that low, cigarette-scratched tone she'd taken on. "Have *you* let *your*self process *your* grief?"

She'd grab her face, give me that old injured look, then waddle back to her room, a bottle of wine in her clutch, ribbons of smoke trailing behind her.

I don't tell her, but I'm trying. I don't tell her I'm worried I might not be able to cry anymore. I don't tell her that, on hot days, I go out and stand barefoot on a steel manhole cap in front of the trailer, wait until I'm near sure my soles will bleed. I don't tell her I press my ear to the bedroom wall at night, hear her whimper herself to sleep. I don't tell her I lie in bed picturing my old man the last time I saw him, slumped over on the toilet with a bullet hole in his head. I don't tell her nothing helps. I don't tell her that no matter what pain I force myself to feel, no matter what mangled memory I drag up, I can't force out a single tear.

Wednesday's back, and I'm sitting in Jimmy Dodge's living room again. His folks still aren't running the AC. It's a furnace in here. Mrs. Dodge passes out snacks, that same crooked smile on her face, then takes a seat in the back.

Coach Tarp's face flashes red. "Accept Christ into your heart." It comes out like an order. He might as well be telling us to crank out twenty push-ups. "Imagine you're in a big building that's burning up. A fire truck pulls up out front. You gonna say, 'Hey, firefighter, sir, no thanks, not me'? That fire's the whole world. It's one big building up in flames."

He pauses, fixes his look on someone up front. A few students fidget in place. "Jesus, he's your firefighter. You're just too dense to see it."

Mrs. Dodge is on her feet, clapping. "Amen, amen."

Someone in a middle row shouts, "Amen."

The door groans open behind me. When I twist back and see Al stepping in, a half hour late, he slams a foot against my ass. It's quick and hard, sends a shock up my spine. He grins. "My bad."

Al finds a spot up front, cramps himself between others. He's a jerkoff. Ever since he came to town in the second or third grade, he's made a mission out of giving kids who won't hit back a hard time. I imagine a knife plunged into his chest, a screwdriver lodged in his neck. But someone yawns and Coach Tarp slams a hand on the little podium. He raises his voice. "Compassion."

Next Wednesday, we're a month out from summer break. Coach Tarp runs his finger through his hair. I wonder how much he's lost since the last time he checked. Everyone gets seated. The sermon starts. The way Coach tells it, we're all sinners, each and every one of us. We need to change course. But there's hope, he says.

Al's up front, elbowing his buddy in the flank. They laugh, plant their hands over their mouths to muffle it.

Coach Tarp ignores them. "We don't have much time left." He smiles something angry. "Any day now, hellfire will burn through the ground beneath us. Chaos comes next. Pandemonium. Cheating. Lying. Robberies. Killing. That's why I want to talk about compassion today. If you haven't got right with the Lord yet, it's time. Right now. It's time."

Coach Tarp bangs on. I tune him out. Kids appear up front, weep. Prayer group ends and I set off for home. Halfway back to the trailer park, I fish a cigarette from my shirt pocket. It's cracked in the middle, a broken bone. I tear the top half off and puff what I can. Gray smoke curls in front of my face. There's hope, I hear Coach Tarp saying. Fucking prove it, I think.

A couple weeks pass. Ma stops asking about my grief. She gets back from work, plants her ass in front of the TV. We only exchange a few words now and then. The most I hear her say comes out in mumbles after she thinks I'm already asleep.

The second to last Wednesday of the school year, Coach Tarp's still hung up on compassion. But his tone's different, softer. "Funny thing about the Lord is he isn't stubborn," he starts. "He'll forgive you alright. You just have to let him in. What's that called?"

No one offers an answer at first, so Coach Tarp prods. "C'mon now. You know what I'm talking about. What's that called?"

A pale hand shoots up somewhere in the front. Whoever it belongs to lets it fall just as quick. Coach Tarp clears a knot of frustration from his throat. "It's compassion. Right? Compassion?"

He ends his sermon. A line forms at the head of the living room. Mrs. Dodge's sitting in a lawn chair she's set up to the side. She rocks back and forth, smiles. One by one the volunteers take their spots. They recall Christ battering into their souls. All around me, football players, girls from the volleyball team, let tears stream down their faces. In their telling, their souls rambled. Glided up and down the streets around town. Shivered across the Piggly Wiggly parking lot. Drifted past the soft, purple glow of the football stadium's lights.

My guts tighten. I can hardly stand it. What have they lost? And who gives a shit about it, anyway?

Jimmy Dodge's turn comes. He scratches his neck, nervous. He says he got drunk, smoked cigarettes, pocketed twenties from his mom's purse. Traded Adderall for a hand job. Mrs. Dodge places a hand over her mouth.

Coach Tarp leans forward, nods. “But I’m so grateful,” Jimmy says. “Who knows? I could’ve ended up in jail. But the Lord’s looking over me.”

Coach Tarp slaps his hands together. “That’s right. Once you start headed down that path, could take you somewhere you don’t want to be.”

Jimmy takes his time. He thanks God, his parents. He thanks Coach Tarp, his classmates who turn out for the prayer group every week. “My parents did everything so that I could get it together.” He ticks off a list of the gifts the Lord has given him: “The glory of his grace, a place in heaven, a starting spot on the football team.”

Yeah, yeah, I think. I could throw up hearing it all, but everyone’s got their faces warped in what must be sympathy. Then, it rips into me like a gunshot. I know what waits ahead. A lifetime of floating around town, from the trailer park to Piggly Wiggly, from the Piggly Wiggly back to Ma conked out on the couch.

I scan the room for a distraction. Mr. Dodge steps out of his office, unfolds a lawn chair next to his wife. They lean forward, bob their heads at one another now and then. I remember Ma alone at home, on the TV the same *Jeopardy* reruns she used to watch with my old man. I remember the way they tangled into one another on the couch. Mr. Dodge clasps Mrs. Dodge's hand, then swings his other arm around her.

I look away. My stomach aches. My heart knives my ribs. I raise my hand to ask for a breather. Al beats me to it. "Coach Tarp. Russ and me—" He nods at his friend next to him. "We need a moment to take it all in."

Coach Tarp, for the first time since I've come to prayer group, makes a face that looks like it's meant to show support. "It's a lot to process, isn't it, boys?"

Al flattens his own face. "A whole lot, sir."

I get up from my spot, step toward the entryway. I search for an explanation, but no one notices me. As the door shuts, I hear Coach Tarp saying something to the others. It's an awful tough sight, a miserable old fuck who gets duped that easy.

Streetlights burn hard in the dark. Trees cast shadow veins on the pavement. I cross the street and sit beneath an old sycamore, light a Marlboro. Al and Russ plod outside, then disappear around the side of the house.

A few minutes pass and they appear in the yard again. Walking toward Coach Tarp's Buick, they're laughing. Al's using the bottom of his shirt to cup something. He wedges whatever it is beneath the driver side door handle.

"That's fuckin' gross," Russ says.

Al laughs again. "Dog shit in the fingernails."

I can't say I do what I do next for Coach Tarp. Who knows why anyone really does anything? Who knows if anyone really does anything for anyone else. But I'm tearing ass across the street, hurtling headfirst toward Al. I'm in the air, the grass green and shadowed beneath me. My face crashes into Al's ribcage first. I'm scrambling to my feet, clutching for shirt collars. Swinging wide, clawing, missing. Stumbling, flat on my ass. Eating a fist to the face, then another.

Al punts me hard in the ass. Russ spits in my hair. Pain shoots sharp and fast through my sides. Dirt finds its way between my teeth. When they're done, I look up at the sky, black and purple and so low I can hardly breathe. I lie there for a long time, listen. Al and Russ laugh, go back inside. If anyone in there's crying loud enough to hear, the throb in my ears silences it. I get up and dust off my knees, turn toward home. A hot breeze rushes me. I spit a mouthful of blood onto the pavement. I pack my shirt pocket. The last cigarette I took off Ma's gone.

On the walk back, the stars blink. Clouds smash into one another. The night unfolds like a sheet. I cross an empty golf course. My shoes squish on damp grass. I track footprints across the Piggly Wiggly lot. I turn down the last bend, follow the unpaved road back to the trailer.

Ma's on the couch, snoring. I'd normally leave her, but she's so thin, it takes almost no work to heave her up. She groans, mumbles. I get her to the bedroom, kiss her forehead. I know I ought to do this kind of thing, some little act of kindness, when she's awake, but something's wrong with me.

In the kitchen, I grab a dishrag, then wipe away the wine Ma's spilled on the coffee table. I kick off my shoes, sit on the couch. There's a *Jeopardy* rerun on the TV. A woman guesses the wrong word and her winning's tick down to nothing. I switch the channel, and a cowboy takes a bullet to the chest.

I remember the day we moved to the trailer park, a few weeks after my old man went. We loaded the car with whatever we could fit, then tossed the rest in the dumpster behind the Piggly Wiggly. Ma gassed it and we headed out past the edge of town. She swung a hard right down a dirt road that cut through a field of waist-high weeds, all potholes. A box of my clothes bounced around in the back. A Diet Coke can full of her cigarette butts spilled at my feet. Kids ran in the field, making wide circles. They hurled stones at each other. Ma pulled up to the last house on the last street, tugged the emergency brake.

"A fresh start." She looked like she had more to say, but whatever had knotted up inside her, she couldn't pry it loose.

A commercial for stray animals comes on. I flip it back to *Jeopardy*. The woman's shaking her head now, shocked. I think of my old man turned into nothing but a bunch of dust and bones in the earth. Ma waking up whimpering. I wonder if that's what it's like for Coach Tarp, putting his wife underneath after so many years together, after watching cancer gnash her up. For a second, I can see it all spread out in front of me, all the reasons I ought to feel sorry for a guy like that.

A throb's in my cheek, a spot where Al caught me good. I scrape a smidge of dirt from between my teeth. Each breath rakes my ribs from inside. I try to drag up the worst pain I've ever felt, but it's no use. I turn off the TV. The room clicks. Moonlight moves through the blinds. I stare at the ashtray on the table. There must be twenty, thirty butts in there. I slip my lighter from my pocket, flick it a few times. One of the cigarettes is hardly smoked, partly buried beneath the others. I sit there a long time, waiting for something to happen, before I finally lean forward and dig my fingers into the ash.

2008

Like Christ hacking up a lung—that's how Barn Boy's old Crown Vic sounded when it backfired. We barreled down an old farm road that sliced the night in half. Barn Boy took a slug of Olde English and passed the bottle. The stench of burned oil hung thick inside the car. Clouds troubled the sky. They'd never put up streetlights that far outside of town, and tree-shaped shadows blasted past us on either side.

We were headed one town over to hunt down Christmas deliveries on front porches. This all happened in late 2008, not long after Thanksgiving. We'd spent the morning driving all over town to apply for jobs. Taco Bell, U-Haul, La Quinta Inn. The managers took one look at us and pushed our applications back across the counters, grinned and wished us luck. Barn Boy came up with the idea. He was always cooking up new plans, and he was all beat up about not landing a job. This plan, he said, would get us enough money to skip town. We'd go home to home in the next town, a place where 2008 wasn't happening, and run off with as many Christmas gifts as we could fit in his Crown Vic. We'd sell them on eBay and split the take. I didn't tell Barn Boy, but I didn't want to leave town. I just wanted enough money to get the lights turned back on at the shack my old man had abandoned me in. I planned to stay there until the bank finally sent someone to drag me out.

Winter was sinking its fingers in, and an early cold spell had washed the fields carcass gray. Every time you turned on the TV, the news was playing B-roll footage of sad people clutching their kids' hands in breadlines. The country was coming apart limb by limb, but we kept dragging out of bed each morning because we had no clue if we were hopeless or there was just no hope at all.

Barn Boy now heeled down on the gas, yipped out the window. The road ran rough, and we bounced in our seats. He sucked on a Marlboro Red until it nearly burned down to the filter, then flicked it out the window into the dark. I watched the rearview as the cherry flailed and disappeared.

"Onward," Barn Boy shouted.

"Shit yeah," I joined in.

Barn Boy pulled off the farm road into a neighborhood. He slowed down in front of homes with Audis and Beamers parked out front. I crept trembling up to porches, eyes peeled. We hit five, maybe six streets, but we struck out. He parked for a while, thought. After a while, he said, "Probably nobody's got money for Christmas shit this year."

"Life a tough place to live right now." I hated myself for repeating a line my old man used to recite like some kind of church prayer after a rough day.

"I know another neighborhood over here," Barn Boy said, and he put the Crown Vic in drive.

We pulled onto a single street, a half-mile long, that jutted like an outstretched arm into a field. The homes were weather-damaged and rundown, and although I didn't want to let Barn Boy down, it didn't feel right stealing from places like that. It wasn't until the last house that we spotted a box on the porch. Barn Boy parked a couple lots down. "Go get it," he said.

I surveyed the house, the stray cats perched on the slumped rooftop. "These people look so bad off they might as well be us."

"You sayin' you're not doin' it?"

I fidgeted in the passenger seat. "We shouldn't. Look at that place. These people got hard luck. Besides, by the look of it, I imagine there's guns around in there."

Barn Boy grunted. "You won't nut up," he said, "I guess I'll have to."

He stepped out and inched past the rusted old Chevy 1500 parked out front toward the porch, then tore back toward the Crown Vic with a bulky brown box cradled in his arms.

Parked off the shoulder a couple miles down the farm road, Barn Boy stared through a tear he'd ripped in the package. "You've got to be shittin' me."

"What's the matter?" I said, and peeled back the flap. The downcast face of the Virgin Mary glared back. Barn Boy lobbed the plastic statue into the backseat, tossed the box out the window, and peeled out.

The closer we got back to our town, the more the woods thinned out around us. The wind slapped hard through the windows, shivered us. Whenever Barn Boy slammed around a tight bend, Mary crashed into the back doors. I watched her in the rearview. About three feet tall and hollow, she couldn't clock in at more than four or five pounds. Who hadn't felt that small at least once in their lives?

Fields fanned out for miles on either side. We rolled

up and down the farm roads until Barn Boy slammed on the brakes and skidded onto the shoulder. He slugged me in the arm, softly. "I've got an idea."

"Because the last one went so well?"

"Fuck off. We'll take this Virgin Mary to Pastor Martin's."

Pastor Martin taught our world religion course at the high school years back, and like most people in town, he'd done something that'd rubbed Barn Boy raw.

"You call that an idea?"

"It's a prank, asshole."

"But what's the prank of it?"

"We'll go find more Virgin Marys. A whole army of them. Stand them all up in Pastor Martin's yard. He'll come out and think it's a goddamn miracle."

"I don't know. Doesn't make sense."

Barn Boy ignored me, threw the Crown Vic into drive, and heeled down on the gas. And there I was sitting shotgun, the Virgin Mary riding bitch.

Everyone called him Barn Boy. His ma supposedly gave birth to him in the splintering old barn behind their house. That's how the story went, at least. That she dropped him out right there, mice and farm cats watching on as his old man thrust in an arm and yanked him out by hand.

Most of us were too young, had too little sense, to question a claim that strange. Anyway, people in this town liked to bullshit. Barn Boy never spoke about it. He just answered to the name like it matched the one on his birth certificate. Plus, his old man passed away in 2005, his ma a year later to the day, and he had no brothers or sisters. There was no way to confirm one way or another.

He'd been there for me when we buried my ma, even as my old man started to loathe me as some kind of reminder of the wife he lost. Any time the pantry was empty, Barn Boy appeared on my front porch bearing canned foods—beans, pears, hash—and Olde English. He let me ride around in his Crown Vic, no money to chip in on gas, and sleep on his bedroom floor whenever my old man left the door deadbolted at home. He never asked for anything in return, and I never did anything worth a shit on his behalf. Barn Boy didn't even give me grief last year when, as I stood in place quivering in the Wendy's parking lot, a group of boys from across town jumped him. He was just good like that, but lately, he'd looked at me with disappointment in his eyes.

Behind us, a pickup flashed its brights. The driver honked the horn twice, pulled right up on our ass. My heart thrashed something wild, and I gripped the door handle hard as I could. Barn Boy, glancing at my tremoring hands, shook his head and said, "It's not that same Chevy."

"You sure?"

The pickup swerved left of us, roared past, and left exhaust clouds behind it, the word FORD impressed on its tailgate.

"Told you."

"You didn't know one way or the next."

"You don't got to be so scared of everything."

A few minutes up the road, Barn Boy let up on the gas. Streetlights stained the pavement yellow. I popped the middle console and took one of Barn Boy's Reds, fired it up. Barn Boy still had Pastor Martin on his mind. He wasn't paying me any attention, so I slipped the rest of the pack into my jacket pocket.

"A sign from God himself." Barn Boy shot me a look like that ought to clear it all up.

"Why the fuck would he think that?"

"He believes all that shit."

"Believes *what* shit?"

"Y'know, religion. Splitting the seas. Clouds parting. An army of plastic Marys in his front yard."

"Never seen that last one in the Bible."

He threw his hands up like me not getting it was wearing him out. "Fuck it. I don't know."

I laughed. "Far as pranks go, it's the dumbest goddamn thing I ever heard. Your parents raise you in the wilderness?" It just came out that way, but I already felt bad. For all I know, he really was born in a barn.

Barn Boy kept silent, stared straight ahead. After a while, he cleared his throat and replied matter-of-factly, "They might as well've."

Three weeks earlier, a sedan had pulled up in front of our shack and parked next to the mailbox at the bottom of the drive. A man stepped out in a pressed white button-up and a dotted tie. He was young, not much older than me. A real asshole, by the look of it. He marched up the dirt path cutting the yard in two, papers in his clutch. The sun shone pale and tired, and a cold wind swept across the porch. I sized him up through the screen door. "We're not buyin' shit."

A smile cut across his face. "Yeah, no shit." He slapped an eviction notice on the door. "You got thirty days. Thank you."

He turned toward his car, and because I was too angry to know what else to say, I hollered at his back, "You're welcome."

My old man was sitting on the couch, using a kitchen

knife to dig dried mud out from the grooves of his boot soles. He stared at me like his eyesight was troubling him. "You dim?"

The next night, my old man emptied the canned foods from the pantry, tossed them in a brown duffle bag along with a couple weeks' worth of clothes. I followed him out to the porch and stood there shivering as he locked the front door on his way out. He fired up his Ford Ranger.

"Can't you leave the key?" I held myself against the cold. "I lost mine. We still got a month, anyhow."

"Probably best you go ahead and figure out what's next. Can't you just stay with a friend 'til you land on your feet?"

"You think I'll land on my feet?"

He stared at his lap, seemed to consider it for a moment. "Probably not."

"Well, can't I just come with you?"

"You wouldn't like it there."

He threw the pickup in reverse, started inching backward down the drive, then turned onto the dirt road and made off. I slipped out of my T-shirt, wrapped it around my hand, and punched through the living room window. I stayed in my bedroom for a week with the space heater blasting until someone showed up and cut the electricity.

Then, I still stayed there shivering under a mound of blankets until a couple days later, when a technician came out and cut the phone line.

"Sorry," he said.

I was standing at the open window, watching. "I'll bet."

He glared at me with what I guessed was real concern. "Say, man, you alright?"

"Everybody's bound to get that question now and then."

"Yeah." He scratched his head. "So what?"

"And ninety-nine motherfucking times out a hundred, the answer'll always be no, that's so what."

The Crown Vic growled past a Chevron advertising 87 octane at $3.23 a gallon. Barn Boy plowed through a red light. The radio flashed five after midnight, and though we'd spent our entire lives in town, we'd put back too many Olde Englishes to remember where Pastor Martin's house was.

"Bet it's a fancy house," Barn Boy said. He reached down, snatched a bottle that was rolling around beneath his feet on the floorboard, and tipped it back. "Wherever it is."

"Maybe so," I said, though I had my doubts. Cancer spent years dismembering the pastor's wife, same way it tore my ma to pieces ten years back, and I knew nobody—not even a man of the Lord—got a discount at the hospital.

"Any sip left there in that O.E.?" I asked.

"Naw. Was just piss, anyhow."

We sat parked in the Wendy's lot. The stereo was too low to make out anything. Every now and then, a car funneled into the drive-thru lane and rounded the backside of the building. Crickets screamed nearby. Barn Boy grabbed a change cup from the holder and shook it around. "All pennies," he said.

"Welcome to Wendy's," a lady's voice rasped through the speaker.

Barn Boy turned to me. "You hungry?"

"My Visa's maxed," I told him, but he knew no bank was giving me a credit card.

"Yeah. Same here. Spent all my money on my vacation in Belize."

"What'd the Pastor ever do to you, anyhow?"

Then it all came back to me. The pastor failed Barn Boy in ninth grade because Barn Boy couldn't name even one of the Ten Commandments, and his ma made him quit the football team after that. Still, I didn't say nothing. Part of me wanted him to hear how stupid it sounded out loud. But Barn Boy didn't take the bait.

"Huh," he said, same way he always did when he didn't like a question. "Oh. Nothing really."

Barn Boy got back on the topic of leaving town. He said we should consider Dallas. He wanted a family—a wife and kids, maybe a collie—but couldn't get himself to leave on his own. "We could get us a couple of wives who're already best friends," he said. "Houses on the same street. Raise us a flock of Peewee All-Stars."

Sad as shit, a grown man who couldn't make something as simple as skipping town work out. Still, Barn Boy didn't do himself any favors. He dumped all his unemployment into that Crown Vic. It was a '92, real sleek, and although he'd spent a grip on a slick black paint job and eighteen-inch rims, he'd never put a penny into the engine.

"Fuck it," he said. "Why not?"

"Take off?" I scratched my beard, and tiny twists of hair fell from my face, floated down. "Yeah right."

"You act like I'm askin' you to go halfway across the world. It's just Dallas. Hour's drive, tops."

"How am I meant to take care of the house from Dallas?"

"Take care of the house? You don't got no house, bud. Not for long."

"You too big a pussy to go on your own?"

Barn Boy's face contorted. "You don't join, I'll damn well go on my own."

"Why're you so eager to up and leave, anyhow?"

"Why're you so fuckin' afraid of leaving?"

It wasn't that he was wrong, but anger writhed up inside me. I thought of the shack. My ma was born there, inherited it when her folks passed, breathed her last breath there. "Why're you so fuckin' afraid of staying? You scared of living among ghosts at your place? Your old man and your ma show up and haunt you?"

Barn Boy peered at me. He sat silently, knuckles kneading the air in front of him. After a while, he leaned back in his seat with resignation. "If I done you wrong somehow," he said, and shook his head, "if I ain't been there for you, you can just tell me I been a shitty friend."

Shame shot down in my stomach like a corpse pitched into a deep body of water. I thought hard about what to say, but whatever words were left didn't matter, not anymore.

We sat there for half an hour. Barn Boy didn't say a word. I glanced at the rearview. Mary was on her side, staring back. I could hardly meet her eyes. Barn Boy wasn't wrong. I'd said too much, and now tried to snap him out of it.

I slapped the dash. "Wait. Isn't it a matter of fact Pastor Martin lives off 14th?"

Barn Boy wouldn't look my way. He let out the sigh of someone who'd put his lot in with a partner in crime that let him down one too many times. "Who gives a shit, honestly?" He pulled the car lighter from the dash, searched for his smokes. "Where the fuck did my pack go? Man, fuck it. I'll drop you off and head home."

But before he could throw it in reverse, the old Chevy 1500 swung into the lot and skidded to a stop behind us, blocking the Crown Vic in.

"The fuck?" Barn Boy laid on the horn, wrenched his head out the window. "You mind?"

A man dropped out the passenger seat. He had on one of those beige Carhartts only farmers wore. He flashed a flashlight around in Barn Boy's backseat, even though the parking lot lampposts had the interior lit up bright as a hospital.

"Tell me." He had a voice like sheets of sandpaper scratched together. "That belong to y'all?"

Barn Boy didn't like his attitude one bit. "Why? You her father?"

Even in the cold, sweat glossed over me.

"What if I am her father?"

Barn Boy stiffened up, and I could tell he was weighing

whether to get out and scrap. He rolled his knuckles the way he always did when he got worked up, then glanced my way and saw right through me: that same frightened face that had never before bothered to back him up.

He opened his door, got out of the Crown Vic, and stepped chest to chest with the guy. They spoke low in the way people do before it's clear whether someone will throw the first punch or the tension will fizzle. Barn Boy cocked back and tossed a wide haymaker, toppled the guy to the pavement. The man fought to his feet, reached through the pickup window, and came back with a shotgun.

Then, Barn Boy was back in the car, yanking the shifter into drive, gassing it. The carriage grinded over a curb stop, the sound of metal against concrete. In the rearview, the man waved his flashlight around.

"She's ours now, dickhead," Barn Boy screamed out the window, loud as he could.

"Easy, easy," I was telling him. "Easy, Barn Boy."

"You," he said, and as the shifting gear sent the car into a dash, waited a full minute. "You don't say a fuckin' thing to me."

We were halfway back down the farm road when the OIL LOW light ticked on. Barn Boy was flooring it. Smoke strained through the vents. I rolled down my window, Barn Boy his, and he leaned out the window to issue another war cry. The smoke had me coughing. Brights lit up behind us. We had a good lead on the pickup, but the Crown Vic's motor started sputtering.

"Son of a bitch's giving out," Barn Boy said, not seeing how obvious that fact was.

He drifted the Crown Vic to a stop on the shoulder, reached for the Virgin Mary in the backseat. "Whatever happens, he ain't getting this."

We flung the doors open, nearly fell out of the Vic. We made it twenty, maybe thirty yards into the woods before the pickup screeched to a halt on the roadside, the sound of gravel kicking up into the brush. Barn Boy had a lead on me even with the Virgin Mary wedged between his arm and his flank. My thighs ached and the briars lashed my arms through my jacket sleeves, but I heaved forward trying to keep up.

Barn Boy glanced back, shouted over his shoulder. "This way'll get us to your place, right?"

"I sure hope so," I said, panting so hard I could hardly hear myself.

The trees gave way to an opening. We paused a beat and fought to catch our breath. The moon crawled out from behind a cloud, baptized the sky a deep purple. For a moment, nothing felt real. I thought I'd been there in that same situation my whole life. We broke out laughing. Then, Barn Boy stilled himself. Something rustled in the woods, nearer and nearer. Someone shouted something so mangled you couldn't make it out if you had dog ears. Then, we heard what must've been a shotgun cocked. We pushed on into the brush.

"Your house, your house," Barn Boy was saying. His voice came out all tremors. He was practically pleading, the Virgin Mary cradled in his arms like a child. "It's this way?"

I looked at Barn Boy, everything for once clear. Our lives there were pathetic as a goddamn sitcom. For the first time, I saw Barn Boy for who he was—someone who feared a beating like anyone else but had toughened up because he knew I wouldn't. Then, my thoughts crashed down on me from every which way. I was mad as hell at my old man for not living up to his end of the bargain. And I was sadder than ever realizing I should've left with Barn Boy the first time he brought it up, that nothing good was headed our way there.

A shotgun blast cracked the quiet in two. I clamped down on my thoughts. Still, I couldn't tell Barn Boy he was wrong, that we must've gotten turned in circles, that there was no telling which was home. The wind screamed through the trees, my feet concreted to the earth. Another shot sounded off, this time closer.

I took Barn Boy by the shoulder. "You go that way." I flicked my head at the Virgin Mary. "Keep her safe."

"You coming with me," Barn Boy said, but I couldn't say whether it was a statement or a question.

I fumbled in my pocket and found the soft pack, sparked a smoke, and handed Barn Boy the rest. "Where'd you get these?" he asked.

Another shot rang out, and I jogged in its direction, the cigarette hanging from my lips.

"Leave," I said. "Get home. I'll throw him off. Then, we'll go to Dallas."

"I ain't going nowhere without you," Barn Boy shouted.

"You just get out of here," I hollered, and he turned and tore ass the other direction.

I looked up through the gashes in the canopy. Night had beat the sky black and purple. Who could say why, but laughter ached through my sides like someone stabbing their way out of me. Each pull on the cigarette burned my throat. In the clearing up ahead, the man in the Carhartt stepped forward, shotgun raised. I pushed his way through the brush. Briars and branches pulled me each way until I was damn sure I'd come apart limb by limb.

ROOSTER

None of us knew where Rooster'd gotten off to. We mentioned it now and then, over beers at Red's, but we figured he'd gone on a bender. He did that—vanished, then reemerged with a story you could've just boiled down to a fuckup who drank too much. So, when he finally turned up a couple weeks later, we were already tying one on and no one hardly turned to tell him hey.

Rooster's neck was bruised blue, red welts on the sides. "The rope snapped a water pipe in the garage," was the first thing he said. "Imagine that. You think you're going to get relief, and then you're ass deep in a puddle."

We were all twenty-one, twenty-two. It was 2008. The crisis hadn't turned North Texas into just a bunch of breadlines, but the bank had foreclosed on Rooster's family house. His father steered his F-150 off a bridge into Lake Lewisville. For months, Rooster had talked about offing himself too. We didn't take him seriously. Shameful as it sounds now, we all assumed he just wanted attention. Sure, we'd all lost loved ones at some point—an uncle, a grandma, a cousin—but we didn't know real grief. Not like his. Not yet.

"Next time jog a little before you tie the rope to a pipe," Jerry said. He nodded toward the beer gut Rooster had packed on over the last year.

Benny chimed in. "Probably no buildings tall enough in town to throw yourself off." He reached across the table, took one of Rooster's smokes. "Maybe drive into a wall fast as you can."

Rooster rubbed his neck and winced a little, but a smile cracked on his face. "Only problem is I still haven't saved up enough for a ride," he said. "Could be I'll swallow all my old man's antidepressants."

Some college girls appeared at the bar. Red's was a strange spot, one of the few where the students from out of town and people like us, people raised here, gathered under the same roof. Red always kept the stereo too loud—bad music, hair bands and whatnot. We stared at the girls in their frayed denim shorts as they shouted over the music. They ordered a tray of shots, took them back to their frat guy boyfriends. Glasses were slammed on tabletops.

Other locals loitered next to the dartboards, a guy everyone called Dump Truck because of his size and all the lowlifes that kept his company, guarding their besieged patch of territory like it was the Battle of Gonzalez. For our part, we were neither here nor there, glad the college assholes shunned us but with no sympathy for Dump Truck and his band of dickheads, who had a habit of putting too many back and starting fights that ruined whatever passed for a good time in this town.

"Might as well just use a gun," I told Rooster. I still don't know why. Maybe I was trying to join in. Maybe I'd had the thought once or twice myself. Benny shot me a look like he'd help put a bullet in my skull. Jerry shook his head and glared like a father who, for the first time, understood his kid was a fuckup. It didn't strike me as worse than what anyone had said, not even Rooster. But darkness clouded Rooster's eyes. He let out a breath that seemed to drain him of his soul. He fished his wallet out of his back pocket, set a five down on the table, and that was that.

· ·

You'd think we would have changed, but after Rooster's funeral, we kept sitting at the same table at Red's, wearing the same ragged old button-ups and jackets we bought at second-hand stores, making the same jokes.

"This make me a murderer?" I asked.

"Murderer?" Jerry said. He downed his beer, then took mine and tipped it back. "Shit no. Something else."

Benny, stubbing a cigarette, snapped his fingers. "A suicide whisperer."

I never saw it coming with my old man. This was two years after Rooster offed himself. For days, my mom and I sat there in his hospital room. The bullet had entered beneath his chin, shattered the bone under his right eye on the way out. I lost myself staring at the hole in his face, as if it was a crater I could climb down inside and walk around in.

"What a miracle," my mom said, sitting next to the window.

The doctor grunted. "Pretty common, actually." He leafed through the pages on a clipboard.

"What's common?" I asked.

He glanced up from the papers for half a second, almost annoyed, and pressed a finger under his chin. "Getting it wrong. The angle of the gun."

That night, my mom kept watch over my dad, and I walked down to Red's. "Welcome to the club," Benny said. A heart attack had buried his father a few months earlier.

"He ain't dead," I said.

When Benny and Jerry looked at me, confused, I stumbled through the whole explanation, told them about the doctor and the angle of the gun.

My father checked out of the hospital a week later. He never said whether the gun kicked or he hesitated at the last second. Little by little, he got back to whatever was normal now. Even today, I'll walk over to their place and find him in the yard, legs crossed and reclining on a lawn chair. Smoking. Scratching his scar. Staring up at crows on the electrical line. How anyone survives all that only to find pleasure in watching birds drop wet shit on the asphalt, I really can't say.

Not long ago, Dump Truck fucked around and got himself killed. "Suicide by cop," the papers called it, but the jury's still out on that one. I still see Benny and Jerry now and then, though it's tough to find the time. I work the graveyard shift at a Holiday Inn Express. I set off dragging ass toward home around the time the sun's just starting to splash over the horizon. In that strange morning glow, before I even notice the birds singing, I'll be deep into conversation with Rooster by the time I realize I'm mumbling to myself. What does he say? What makes you think you'd even want to know, really?

A fire scorched Red's place last year. The flames collapsed the rooftop, ate away half the facade. Rumor had it Red, behind on what he owed on the place, lit the match. No charges were ever filed. The property sat there in charred ruins for months. When it went to foreclosure, the university snatched it up at a steal. They'll soon flatten what's left of it, put up student housing. Big towers, eight or nine stories apiece. Taller than anything you ever saw in this town.

"No one blames you." Rooster tells me this every morning, always when I'm crossing through the square downtown, too scared to tell him cancer chewed clean through his mom last year, and that was it for his family.

Bad luck was how my own mom described it when I came over for dinner and gave them the news, but my old man didn't say anything. He was poking at his dinner plate with a fork, staring out the window at those crows.

College kids are stepping into the morning light, shielding their eyes. The crows are stabbing their beaks at each other, fighting over whatever scraps of food they've set upon. Rooster clears his throat. Truth is, I tune him out. It doesn't matter what he thinks. Not anymore.

ICE MAN

Ice Man is banging around out in the living room again. He doesn't know it, but he's reminding me why I'm leaving him high and dry. In the kitchen, I've already wiped the counters clean, scrubbed the scum from the steel sink, pulled all the rotten food from the fridge. He's murmuring something I can't make sense of. I snatch a half-empty beer can from the counter, flip it upside down. Suds splash down the drain. A loud bang sounds off in the living room. With all the racket Ice Man makes, I'd just as soon crawl into the garbage disposal and let it chew me up. Patience, I keep coaching myself. I'll be out of here come the end of next week.

I look beyond the breakfast bar, to where Ice Man is digging around between the couch cushions, ravaging the room on a hunt for the remote control. In all the chaos, between his jagged movements, he bumps his head against the wall and shouts. His real name's David, but he earned his nickname for how much crystal he can smoke. How many times has he taken the place apart one piece at a time? Your guess is as good as mine.

I take a couple deep breaths, thinking of the deposit I dropped for a little studio on the outskirts of North Hollywood. Depending on traffic, it's around forty minutes from where we now live in Van Nuys, a part of town expensive enough to bleed you dry but too far from the city to be worth living in. When I first stopped by to check the new apartment out, the toilet leaked and the lights flickered. But Ice Man already keeps me up all night, tearing up whatever he can get his hands on. With what I've already paid, all I need now is a couple hundred more bucks to lock down the first and last month's rent—sixteen hundred, all told.

I yank the garbage from the can and the bag bursts. Coffee grounds, beer cans, crusty old paper plates, it all shoots across the linoleum. "Can I get a hand in here?" I say. Ice Man may as well be two counties over.

He's a couple years older than me, twenty-four or twenty-five. "Where the fuck is it?" he shouts, tearing the cloth off the table and firing it at the wall. He turns to me and makes a face like he's surprised I'm here, a look

I've gotten used to over the last two years. "Oh, it's you, Tex," he says. "You're here."

I look at the television screen, little blue creatures tending to their mushroom houses and working in their personal gardens. "*The Smurfs*, huh," I say, walking over to the couch and putting the cushions back in place. "Haven't seen this in years."

"*The Smurfs*?" he says. He clenches his teeth. He falls back on the couch, but immediately flies up to his feet again like he sat on a tack. He scoffs, swaying side to side. He says the cartoon is all communist propaganda. Papa Smurf is Joseph Stalin, Smurfette some lady whose Russian name he stumbles over a few times before giving up. I have no clue what happened to Ice Man during his time in the military, but he picked up a lot of ideas over there, wherever he was. He sees secret messages in everything. Real sinister stuff. Just when I think I've heard it all, he spouts off some new story. He's halfway through a tirade about *The Smurfs* before I realize he's already unpacked this one for me.

Back in the kitchen I survey the mess on the floor. A spider inches over a tiny dune of coffee grounds. Ice Man's still speaking, but I can't follow a word of it. "I gotta turn this shit off," he shouts.

Neither of us has slept in days. Red lines crack all around his pinpoint pupils. His skin is sallow and pockmarked, veins fat and bruised blue through his skin. Stains spread under his armpits. Threads of sweat trickle down his forehead, winking in the sunlight. "This commie bullshit, man, you can't let it in your head." He smacks his palm to his skull a couple times.

"Whoa, whoa, bud. Take it easy. The remote will turn up. 'Til then, just ignore the TV. Or get up and hit the switch on the box," I tell him, but he's already stomping off to the other room, kicking the wall all the way down the hall.

Years ago, I packed up everything I owned, backed my old pickup out of my mom's driveway, and pushed out to Los Angeles. Fresh from high school and sick of hearing my mom talk about my dead brother, I showed up with small dreams. I knew better than to try and get famous. A lot of people head west with big hopes about stardom and wind up doing dick flicks. A job and some quiet would be enough for me. I went home to Texas broke and defeated once. Later, I got the idea to try to get admission to a photography school, maybe land a gig doing photo shoots for rich people one day. But when I came back to California, I ended up renting a room from

Ice Man in the Valley, sloshing around with him in all that the city spits upstream.

Ice Man was clean when I met him. Over time he slipped up on his sobriety and our lives started to bend sideways. He couldn't lock down a job and eventually stopped sending out applications. Some months, the disability check the state sends him—it has to do with whatever's wrong with his head—shows up short, others it doesn't come at all.

When he's on a good one, he can go days without so much as blinking. He stays up all night, loading and reloading his pipe and tinkering with appliances: the dishwasher and the disposal, the toaster and television. I sometimes lie in bed listening while he rearranges the photos and posters on the wall, takes a hammer to the hot plate. He fires up his pipe again and again, and the sharp smell—too chemical to be sweet—is enough to wake me on its own, washing right through the walls. On bad nights I swear I can hear his teeth grinding from all the way back in my bedroom.

I make eight fifty an hour at GNC, a quarter more than minimum wage, pushing protein and prostate pills off on middle-aged men. Back home in Texas, my mom tells all the neighbors I hit it big out West working in the self-care industry. On the side, I pull in a couple extra hundred bucks a week taking photos of low-rent celebrities and selling them to tabloids and gossip websites. A few months ago, I told my mom I snapped a shot of some bigwig movie star draining his dick in the alley behind a bar. She started spicing up her stories, telling the whole neighborhood I help famous people fix their broken lives.

I wonder what they'd think if they knew how I really live, but mom doesn't need to know I came home last week and found Ice Man scraping a layer of skin off his forearm with a strip of sandpaper. Who wants to hear all that? She's better off not hearing the story of me choking him out to stop him from prying a molar from his mouth with a pair of rusty pliers.

Ice Man says the army taught him how to survive any disaster. The way he tells it, he could weather a hurricane. He could survive societal collapse, nuclear war, famine. Me, I worry he might go too far and really hurt himself, maybe even die—who knows? It's not like I don't know he's aching. But he can't be helped, and I can't keep on footing the bill for him.

Ice Man storms back into the living room, tossing aside the newspapers and magazines I've left stacked on the stand in the corner. The couch cushions come next, crashing into the wall and knocking down a PRINCE – PURPLE

RAIN poster. Ice Man's mom gifted him that poster. It's got that old photo of Prince posted up on a motorcycle, a cloud of smoke behind him. One night, when Ice Man was tying one on, he told me how much it meant to him. His mom mailed it to him shortly before she got strung out or died—I couldn't remember which—and that poster was all he had left of her. I pick up the poster and place it on the coffee table. Sunlight shifts through the shades. Shattered glass glitters in the carpet. Ice Man cranks his head to look beneath the couch, doesn't notice the shards sprayed out all around us. It could break your heart, seeing someone that gone. I almost have to turn away.

I ask, "Can you ease a bit up out there? You broke your poster, man."

He shoots me a look and huffs, then heaves the couch up on one end and searches beneath it. I broom the trash into a pile on the kitchen floor and scoop it all into a new bag, twist the top into a tight knot. "I'm off to work," I say. "Enjoy the cartoons."

I open the door and look back. "Bullshit propaganda," Ice Man shouts. He's pointing an accusatory finger at the television screen, but I'm already on my way out.

Sitting on a stool behind the counter, I flick vitamins onto the floor and watch the clock tick away seconds. I've already wasted most of my shift switching the pills in the bottles, replacing the lysine tablets with libido boosters. I snatch a pack of energy pills off the display case and chew a few up. My hands rattle for the next hour. How the meth doesn't melt Ice Man, I can't say.

In the year and a half I've worked here, we never have gotten much business. The store is in a dodgy strip mall at the edge of Canoga Park. The crosswalk guards pick-pocket you. The dope dealers are all plainclothes police, and the uniformed cops sell smack. Not many people around here think about multivitamins.

As soon as I save up the rent money, I'll hand in my two-week notice, tell the manager how stupid he is for running a health store in a neighborhood where you can't walk down the street without getting mugged or arrested. On workdays, I hide my cash in my sweaty sock.

In North Hollywood, I'll be closer to the action. I'll make contacts, maybe even go legit. I might be the real deal one day, a sought-out photographer doing shoots for actors and rap stars, the kind of work my mom could really brag about.

For now, the pills have got me smoking like a busted oven. I nearly burn through a pack of Parliaments. My phone dings. It's a message from Steven Nuy. He's an editor at Hollywood Whispers, a website that made its name for photo-shopping pictures of celebrities: nip slips, up-skirts, they turn any innocent accident they can into a national scandal.

"Look for some *Real World* washout at The Chaser?" the message reads. He means a bar in West Hollywood. "In half an hour. Two hundred bucks in it."

I fire up my last smoke and think about it for a moment. I need to start packing, but I need the cash more. "On it," I write back. I count the bills in the register and scrawl STEPPED OUT FOR FAMILY EMERGENCY on a sheet of paper. The strip mall security guard eyeballs me as I lock up and tape the note to the front door, but it doesn't matter. "Yeah, yeah," I shout at him.

"What?" he says.

"Call the manager for all I care."

I spend an hour hunting around behind bars on a hunch, juking junkies and winos, before I spot my guy. His hair is messy in an intentional way, his shirt pressed. The light from the lamppost blinks off his silver watch. His jacket is slick and loose on his thin bones. His dress shoes have big, shiny buckles.

He looks different than he did on MTV, but that was five, six years ago. Rumor has it he's got connections to black business, real rough people, all underground. Ever since his housemates voted him off the show, the tabloids have been running stories about his coke addiction. It shows. His eye sockets are sunken, his face yellow, and a rim of raw, reddened skin wraps around his right nostril. But there's no mistaking his face.

He shoves his hand halfway down a bartender's blouse, crawls the other up underneath her apron. I lean against the wall and make myself small, take a couple photos. The chorus of cars honking nearby and women screaming somewhere far away drowns out the sound of my shutter snapping. I think of the cash I'll make off this and tremble, I'm so excited. My shadow sprawls out on the pavement beside me, shivers when my body shakes.

An old Pabst Blue Ribbon can—that's what gives me away. I step on the can, hear it crunch. He whips his head in my direction. I dive behind a dumpster, but it's too late. He's on me in less than a second, throwing his arms every which way and screaming *what the fuck* this and *what the fuck* that.

He shoves me and I tumble back onto a pile of trash bags. His knee crashes down on my sternum. Some kind of jealousy wells up within me when I catch a whiff of the bartender's perfume on him. He slaps, spits, says he'll kill me. But I move quickly. I duck, roll, twist. Each time he snatches for my camera, he comes back empty-handed.

I make it to my feet, point at the bartender, and shout, "Oh, my god. Is she alright?"

I'm halfway down the alley before he realizes I've made a run for it. He takes off, huffing behind me, but I hang a couple corners and his footsteps grow distant until they eventually fade away. Behind a dumpster I crouch and try to catch my breath.

I check the photos—framed nicely, good use of shadows, quality composition. There are at least a dozen photos on my memory cards back at the apartment, waiting to be sold. I do the math in my head. Enough cash to drop a check off at the management company next week. I realize my wallet is gone, it must have fallen out of my pocket. But it's OK, the wad of cash is still in my sock, like a growth on my foot.

I close my eyes and imagine my new life, try to remember what a full night of sleep feels like. Around me, trash spills from the dumpster: dirty diapers and half eaten vegetables, all rotten. The night hums, humidity thick in the air. The stink soaks my skin. That's alright. Goodbye, Ice Man. California turns you cruel like that, I think, and a rat skitters over my sneaker.

Ice Man pops open a Keystone Light. He chokes down a mouthful and goes on at length about how good a roommate I am, speaking so fast I worry his heart will stop. "I'm going to pay you back for all you've done. Even these beers," he says, motioning toward the thirty-pack on the coffee table. He couldn't pay me back if he wanted, but he gets like this when he drinks, makes promises he can't keep. He picks a pock on his arm, squeezes out a drop of blood.

I picked up the thirty-pack on the way home, half wanting to celebrate my escape, half feeling guilty. He cracks open one beer after another, handing me a can each time he grabs a new one for himself.

Nine, ten beers deep, my head starts hurting. I stand and kick the cramps from my legs, but I sit back down when Ice Man starts unfolding a sheet of tinfoil, readying himself for a long night. He wields the razor blade slowly and with care, and I think back to my mom spending all day in the kitchen the day before I left, dicing onions and peppers and slow-roasting pork flank. "You need a good home meal before you set off. God knows how long it'll be 'til your next," she said, but I didn't think much of it then.

"It's like a ceremony," I say now, and Ice Man nods, quiet for once.

"Learned this in the military."

"They teach you how to chop up meth in the military?"

He looks at me, all offended. "They teach you how to take your time and do things right. They teach you the process matters as much as the outcome."

He sounds like a cheap motivational speaker, but what he's saying makes sense. "I understand," I reply. And in a way, I do. It's the least confusing comment he's made in months.

I jolt awake sitting upright in bed, slick with sweat and snagged in sheets, not sure how I got here. The clock flashes five. My blinds are shut tight. A bird chirps outside my window. I remember the time when a neighbor and I, still in high school, sniffed ourselves stupid with crank, staying up until the birds broke day, tweeting us into a terror. Ice Man is still up out in the living room, banging on something. I roll over and bury my head beneath the pillow, but he doesn't let up.

I creep over and press my ear to the bedroom door, hoping to figure out whether whatever he's breaking will come out of my security deposit. It thuds and cracks, thuds and cracks, until the noise suddenly stops.

Walking down the hall to the living room, I spot the writing Ice Man's scrawled in black Sharpie on the wall, all in rigid capital letters: PRINCE – PURPLE RAIN. There's even a little stick figure with squiggles for curly hair, sitting on a little stick motorcycle with big wheels, and scribbles meant to be smoke, I guess. Then, I see a guy, a real rough type sitting on the couch. He's smiling in a way that makes me uneasy.

"You got a friend over, Ice Man?" I say, but he says nothing. He's sitting on the carpet hugging his knees, childlike. Sleeving the sleep from my eyes, I notice a blue bulge beneath his right eye, a big gash on his eyebrow.

"We only just met," the man says, "but yeah, you could say we are friends, aren't we?" He nudges Ice Man's shoulder with the sole of his boot. "Aren't we?"

"Friends, yeah," Ice Man says.

"How much he owe you?" I ask.

"Nothing."

"So, what's this?" I say. "A robbery?"

"You better watch who you call a thief." I notice the hammer in his right hand.

"That's what this is, isn't it? You came to steal?"

"You're the thief, buddy."

He raises his other hand, holding up my wallet. He sets the hammer in his lap, pats the wallet on his palm a couple times like it's a pipe he wants to pound me with. "You like to take photos, that right?" he says.

I ignore the question, instead watching Ice Man sniffle. "You OK, Ice Man?" I say, but he won't look directly at me. He squeezes his eyes shut like it's all too much to see.

The man clears his throat in a way that makes him seem older than he looks, which is about thirty-five. He's got on a fake-looking leather jacket, and his shirt is only buttoned-up three quarters to the top, revealing a patch of tightly curled chest hair. "We're going to get rid of these photos, alright," he says, his voice confident in a way that shows you how rough he can get, if he wants. "And then I'll give you an ass beating—nothing too serious, just so I can be sure you've learned your lesson. And then we'll never see each other again, you and me."

The man moves the hammer from his lap and fishes a memory card from his pocket, pinching it between his thumb and his index finger, and tells me here's what's going to happen: He's going to watch while I delete all the photos I took of a certain famous someone, someone who has plenty of friends I should worry about, not just him, because he's perhaps the most reasonable of them all, and then he'll be out of our hair. I will never take photos of the certain famous someone again, he adds, because they'd be the last photos I ever took.

The man stands up to walk my way. "Let's get your laptop," he says, but Ice Man springs to his feet behind him, snatches up the hammer. It all slows down now, moves dragged-out in frames, Ice Man cranking his arm back, whacking the man on his head, driving him toward the entrance. I fling open the door and Ice Man shoves him out with all the force he can summon. The man hits the pavement like a sack of garbage. I slam the dead bolt into place.

Stunned, I stand there for a few moments. There's a splatter of blood on the carpet, soaking in. Even from inside, the man snorts, chokes on his own breath, so loud we can hear everything.

Ice Man picks up the memory card from the floor. He hands it to me. "You're supposed to be the smart one here," he says. "What did you do this for?"

"Why'd you let him in? What were you thinking?" A wave of anger rises up inside me, washes my heart down into my stomach. I could kill him. I look at the hammer, still there on the floor, and imagine his face flattened, flesh opened.

"Because he knocked."

"He knocked? Because he knocked on the door? That's why you let him in?"

He winces for a moment, looking wounded, and then his face turns stern. "That sort of thing can get you in trouble, Tex."

"Hundreds of dollars on this memory card," I say, waving it at him. "Weeks and weeks of work, and I almost lose it all because someone knocked on the door and you're too dumb to not let him in?"

I snatch the hammer, white-knuckle it.

He seems to understand where my thoughts are, and a look of resignation appears on his face. But then he grabs my shoulder, fastens his fingers into the flesh. "Be careful. This kind of thing gets people killed. You can't die, man. Don't do that to me."

I try to read Ice Man's face, but there are no messages in it, nothing sinister. Just fear. I have two minds, maybe a hundred. I think hard for a moment, feel something sharp snap in my chest.

"Okay," I say. "Break it."

"Break what?"

I toss him the memory card and hand off the hammer. He winds up a little bit and gives me a look meant to ask whether he's understood me correctly. Then, it clicks for him. He brings the hammer down hard on the memory card, so hard that a floorboard cracks down under the carpet, a loud, splintery crack sound. Crouching, I flick away what's left of the memory card. The fragments, little, plastic shards, fan out everywhere. Ice Man is in the kitchen, reaching for the broom, when I say forget it. Later, I tell him. Tomorrow or the next day. I've got nowhere else to be.

Ice Man looks like he's got something to say, but nothing comes out. "Try and get some rest," is all I manage. When the tears gather on his face, I can't help but break eye contact. I try hard to get a glimpse of the future, some road out of here, but no matter how hard I try, I can't see past the mangled look on Ice Man's face, the couch cushions sideways on the floor, the light glittering off little specks of glass.

THE HAN GIL HOTEL

I was riding shotgun in Ron's old Nissan. We had once taken turns on the same needle, but years had passed since we'd seen each other. When we graduated high school, I kicked. I left Texas, ran off to Kansas, enrolled at a two-year, relapsed, dropped out, moved in with a crank head, kicked again, reenrolled, graduated with a history degree, and never once visited home. It took Ron a lot longer to get clean, from what I'd heard.

We were headed to a bar downtown. He lifted a beer to his lips and killed half of it, then flipped the turn signal three or four exits too early. I asked what the detour was all about. He used to be a good time, real talkative. Now, he just said somewhere. Where, I asked, but he only repeated himself: somewhere.

Ron wedged the beer back between his thighs. Downtown Dallas throbbed against the gray night sky.

Green neon outlined the Bank of America building. Next to it a blue light burned atop Reunion Tower. Fluorescents glowed through the windows of high-rise offices. Fifteen years earlier, we drove this same way, south on US-75, to get our hands on a bag whenever no one in town was holding.

I ended up in Ron's passenger seat after I tracked him down on Facebook. I told him we ought to grab a beer. TOMORROW NIGHT, he wrote. His tone hit me as almost too straightforward, but I'd never been able to read people in person, let alone in text. PICK YOU UP AT THE BUS STATION BY THE BOWLING ALLEY.

I'd sat on a bench watching homeless people step off the bus, faces sweat-soaked and haunted. I had a friend's couch to crash on for at least a few more days, but if the goodwill ran out, I might be in the same boat. Ron pulled up and reached across to open the door. A twelve-pack of Natural Light sat on the passenger seat.

For whatever reason—failure, probably—I'd ended up back home, broke and without work. My mom moved away a long time ago, and ever since she remarried, I hadn't kept in touch. I didn't keep in touch with anyone. I hoped Ron might offer me a spot to sleep for a couple weeks. We had history. We met at the end of elementary school then both joined the baseball team freshman year. Later, when heroin slipped back into the suburbs, we raided DVD collections at house parties and sold the haul to Movie Trading Co. Kids started dying junior year. That didn't dissuade us. We took it as evidence of our ability to survive.

I took a sip of my beer, stared at the Bank of America building and its blaze of fluorescents like little rips in the sky. "What a waste. They keep that shit on all night?"

Ron braked and eased onto the exit toward the frontage road. "The lights?"

I glanced his way. He kept his eyes fixed straight ahead. Gray hair shone around his ears, and his skin had become coarse, his face covered in tiny pocks. He was tall, built like a pickup, but he looked like a strong enough cough might tear him in two. Some guys keep on the junk too long, and they never look right again. He drained the rest of his beer and tossed the can over his shoulder, grabbed another from the middle console and snapped it open.

"How much do they spend on that, I mean." I felt stupid saying something so obvious, but Ron had hardly offered a word since he picked me up. "Lots of hungry people in this city."

He half-scoffed. "It's America." He hooked a right on red and gassed the Nissan west. "Every man for his self."

It wasn't until his third beer that Ron started to liven up. He lit a Pall Mall and passed it to me, then lit another for himself. He jammed his knee to the steering wheel to keep the car steady, then downed the beer and crushed the can in the same motion. I was still nursing my first.

"Can't drink like you used to?"

"Don't try to drink like I used to."

Ron shook his head like I had a lot to learn. He started talking a lot. He ticked off a list of people who'd died while I was gone. With each story, he seemed to wake up a little more. A hotshot put an end to Brandon Edgewood, he said. Brian Monroe couldn't pace himself and went too far. Andrew Rose got himself stabbed on a snatch and run.

I left and never visited for a reason. I'd always thought going home would be too risky, as if just being in the same city as people I used to nod off with would be enough to kill me. I didn't even like thinking about death. I knew it didn't bother some people, that they could accept they'd one day have to die. I didn't think life had some special meaning, but it wasn't about that. It just seemed unfair, how quick it all had to end.

Ron smoked his cigarette down to the filter. He dropped the butt in a beer can. "Who else?" he said, and fired up another smoke. "Chris, what's his name?" He released a chestful of smoke. "Chris Field."

No surprise there. I remembered Chris. He was a nice enough guy, but he started early. In the eighth grade, I walked in on him in a bathroom stall, crushing up the painkillers his mom got after a back surgery. I liked him, though—he'd handed me the husk of a pen and offered me a rail that day—and didn't want to hear the details.

Ron laughed from low in his gut. "Ol' Chris got picked up driving." He ashed in a beer can. "Had junk on him. Withdrawals in the holding cell took his sorry ass."

Ron let out another little laugh, turned down a residential street. I didn't recognize the area. Half the streetlights didn't work. What houses I could make out were small, wood-framed blocks. Whenever Ron let the Nissan drift a bit, the headlights revealed junk scattered in the dirt yards, old car parts, toys, bicycles without wheels. Then a stray dog sprinted in front of the car. Ron swerved and barely missed it. He steadied the wheel with one hand, lifted a beer to his lips with the other.

Unease clotted in my chest. I'd heard about withdrawals killing people, but at the time I left, no one else I knew of had tried to quit. "Withdrawals killed him? Chris?"

"Shit no." Ron laughed again. "They just helped him make the decision. Killed himself in a holding cell. Made a noose out of his shirt, some shit like that. Had two kids. Anyway, natural causes."

"Pretty sure hanging yourself doesn't count as a natural cause."

We passed under a streetlight. Ron tensed his eyebrows, then a smile settled at a slant on his face. "Fuck," he said. "Natural enough."

The residential street spat us out onto Royal Lane. Ron flipped on the radio, then clicked it off. He turned up the AC. Chris Field was still on my mind. I wondered how old his kids were, imagined his old lady—whoever she was—telling them one day.

Ron stopped at a red light. "Here's another good one. Remember Jimmy?"

The light turned green, and he hit the gas. We passed a liquor store. A Bud Light sign flashed in the window. A group of men stood outside, near the dumpster, huddled around one another. Anyone, I thought, could end up like that.

"Jimmy who?"

"Jimmy Dodge."

That name gave me pause. None of them sat right with me, but Jimmy had been straight the whole time we were growing up. Freshman year, his parents hosted the after-school prayer group my mom made me go to after my old man offed himself.

"Jimmy? No shit?"

"Jesus freak like that, he never stood a chance."

"He was a good kid. I mean, he didn't do shit like we did."

"Doubt, my friend," Ron said, a dark glee in his voice. "Those people don't know how to cope. If you can stay sure your life has some kind of special significance in the big, wide world, you'll be alright. Once you let the doubt in, you break hard."

"I don't want to hear no more."

"Not even how he died?"

"Seriously." The words came out sharp. "I don't want to hear it."

Ron was gripping the steering wheel as if he wanted to strangle it. "Fuck you, you don't."

He rattled off how Jimmy came back from college one Christmas and started disappearing on his folks. He went weeks without answering his phone. His parents eventually put the pieces together. They were sweet, naive even, but not blind to everything that was happening in town. They set him up at rehab, some expensive spot for families who can foot the bill. He cleaned up, came out, went dark again.

I pictured Jimmy's mom. She looked like every mother from a family with more money than Ron's or mine. She used to walk up and down the aisles during prayer group and pass out cookies. His father sat in the back, rocked forward and backward during the sermon, such intensity on his face you'd have thought he was witnessing the Resurrection that very moment.

Ron was picking up speed, cut off a Buick. "You know how they found out he died?"

"I don't give a shit how."

"How?"

"I don't want to know." My voice rose with the fear of hearing it said aloud.

"They just kept phoning him," Ron said. "For weeks they rang him up every day. No answer, not ever. Then his phone got disconnected. You know that shit? 'The number you are calling is no longer in service,' or whatever it says." Ron stopped at a red light, peered out over the intersection. "That's how they knew."

"By a phone message?" I said. "He could've just taken off. Maybe he got arrested and had to go away for a bit."

"I guess he could've."

"Could've got clean. Could've went somewhere else, fixed his life."

The edge returned to Ron's voice. "You'd know about shit like that, huh."

I understood how much he held it against me, taking

off. "Not really," I said. "Now explain how a disconnected phone equals death in your world?"

The light turned green. "I guess you're right," Ron said, easing the car into the intersection. "I mean, you ran off and changed numbers, and look at you—alive and doing great. Regular success story, you are."

Maybe Ron had changed. He used to be caring, or what passed as caring in the small world around us. He'd shaken me awake one night when I was passed out on his bedroom floor, choking on my own vomit. When everything came into focus around me, I saw tears in his eyes. He snatched a T-shirt from the floor and wiped my face.

But maybe the problem was that, after all these years, he hadn't changed nearly enough. He could also, back in high school, shock you with how callous he could be. One night senior year, Billy Barker took too many whippets and fell flat on his face at a party. His body was twitching. Everyone crowded around him, nervous and scratching their noses. Ron, a bulge of DVDs stuffed in his waistband, threw his hands up and shouted, *Let the weak rest.*

Ron turned into an empty parking lot. He parked diagonally across two spots, finished the last of his beer. I stared at the side of his skull and thought. He pressed his front teeth hard into his bottom lip. He had something he wanted to say, I could tell, but whatever it was, he didn't want to say it yet.

It could have been any other abandoned motel in northwest Dallas, but the sign jogged my memory: THE HAN GIL. Long arms of rooms reached out from an X-shaped building. Someone, probably city workers, had barricaded the entrance. You could make out the spots beneath the windows where the air conditioning units had been torn off. At the far end of the lot, a group of drifters—just shadows, really—passed a cigarette back and forth between them, the cherry flaring in the dark.

Ron opened his door. "You remember this place?"

"Wish I didn't."

"I'm glad I remember it."

We'd only driven down there once, a week or two ahead of graduation. Ron and I had spent the evening with a few other guys. We wanted a bag, but the guy we usually bought from got himself arrested while selling at the bowling alley. Only Ron and I were desperate enough to go hunting for a fix in Dallas.

Ron lit another smoke. "What do you remember, exactly?"

"That clerk."

He grunted. "Clerk? I don't remember no clerk. Why do you remember that?"

"We were going in over there"—I pointed at the front entrance, now nailed shut with scrap wood—"and I kept thinking he'd stop us or warn us to not go in there. Or maybe I was just hoping he'd do something. At least frown and shake his head, anything. I mean, we were kids walking into a place like that."

"I don't see why he'd care. Probably'd seen worse. People got killed here later. Maybe some had already been killed here. But later, it got bad. They wound up full of water and weighed down in the Trinity River."

That brought back a hazy image, a pistol on the nightstand next to the lamp in the room where we handed over a wad of bills we'd gotten for a stack of old horror DVDs at Movie Trading Co. A woman passed out face-down on the bed was so thin I thought she was dead. Hair blanketed her face. But the guy who sold to us—I couldn't remember his face at all.

Ron walked over to a door, tried to pull back the wood nailed to the frame. He walked back to the Nissan, popped the trunk, and came back with a crowbar. It took him three or four heaves, but he busted the sheet of wood off the door and found it unlocked. "C'mon."

Moonlight filtered through the gap in the door, revealed a scatter of debris inside the room. Amid the shadows lay old T-shirts, wadded-up underwear, crumbles of napkins and cellophane. A lone syringe was on the nightstand, next to it an overflowing ashtray with a rusted old spoon in it. Ron flipped the light switch, but the electricity had been cut. He said over his shoulder, "Cops finally shut it down. Years later. Some kids from Coppell died after they scored here. It was in the papers for a while. I guess you wouldn't have seen that news."

"No, I didn't see that news. I was already gone." I stepped into the guts of the room, cautious, as if I might wake someone. The smell of decay nearly gagged me.

"Guess you were, weren't you?" Ron lit a cigarette, left the lighter aflame, and surveyed the room. "They're meant to bulldoze it. Then what? No more junk around here? Everything's fine, all good? A guy like you takes off and keeps clean, doesn't have to bother thinking about this place anymore."

I regretted what I said next before the words left my mouth. Ron was hurt, I could see that much, but his jabs were too much. It all came out too fast, too defensive. "And what about you? You kicked, last I heard. You think keeping this shit tied to your ankle like an anchor does any good for anyone?"

Even veiled in shadows, Ron's face seemed to burn red. He stepped so close to me I could smell the beer on his breath. The next moment stretched on for what felt like hours. His fists balled. I made knots of my hands. We both stood there, our breath ragged, waiting to see who might throw first. But we waited too long, and finally, a sad smile came to Ron's face. "You don't understand a goddamn thing, do you?"

"What exactly is it you're so fuckin' hot on me understanding? You mad that I didn't stay here? Well, good fuckin' thing I didn't. If I stuck around, I'd just be another sad sack who couldn't keep a belt off his arm. I'd be a star in one of your goddamn stories. That what you want?"

Ron flicked his cigarette into my chest. "You think that's it? I wanted you here tying off?" He stepped into a shaft of light coming in from outside. His eyes welled up. "You fuckin' left me. We were friends. Best friends. You took off and didn't bother glancing back, and I was stuck here strapped to a chair with a front-row seat of everyone we knew getting buried."

I wanted to tell him it wasn't what he thought, that I just tried to survive the only way I knew how. But when I opened my mouth, the words scabbed in my throat. He swiped a hand across his eyes, wiped it on his shirt, and I had to turn away. I looked across the room, sat on the bare mattress staring at the wall. A few minutes passed in silence. Someone had scrawled HELP on the wall. "You're right, Ron." I closed my eyes. A rush of blood whooshed in my ears. "Listen, we can still go grab a beer, talk."

I stood up and turned around, but there was no one there. I stepped outside into the night. A woman was walking along the sidewalk, stamping in tall heels and pulling her skirt down her thighs. A man in a baseball cap dragged his dog on a leash behind him. A police car shot past, an ambulance wailing not far behind it. Over the murky outlines of homes across the street, the glow of downtown stained the night sky, and in the Han Gil's parking lot, there were only shadows, weighing down so heavy I thought they might suffocate me.

Weeks went by. I made plans to leave again, but I had no income and there were no jobs. People were getting laid off right and left. I never said it aloud, but I'd accepted that life had put me back here. I checked my Facebook now and then, but Ron had deactivated his account. It turned out I didn't need him, anyway. I found couches to crash on, managed a week at one guy's house, a month at another's. Each morning, I walked to the Home Depot and waited for someone who needed cheap day labor. I mowed lawns, trimmed trees. I built fences, dug ditches. I eventually saved up enough for a studio, a cramped one-room place with a pullout couch and no kitchen. It got to where I couldn't sleep without drinking, and I spent most of what was left over after rent at the bar.

I called old friends and asked about Jimmy Dodge. "Heard he died," they told me. "Sad story." But it still didn't sit right with me. One night, I found his parents' phone number online.

"Dead?" his mother said from the other end, almost surprised at first. "You could say that. Might as well be."

A lump swelled up in my throat. "Mrs. Dodge, do you know where he is?"

"I'm the last person he'd tell."

"You got no idea at all?"

"I haven't had an idea in a long time," she said, her voice impatient. "I don't know. He used to go to that bar off Main Street. Used to run up my credit card bill there."

"You think he's still going—" I started, but the phone clicked dead, and whenever I rang again, no one answered.

June found me in the bar on Main Street nearly every night. It wasn't until the first week of July that Jimmy Dodge walked in. I'd almost given up hope. He stamped right up to the bar and ordered a shot of Maker's Mark. I was tying one on, and when I spotted him, I had to choke back vomit. I walked over, fell into the barstool next to him, and told him the story. He smelled of dirt and sweat. His skin looked like damp paper. He scratched the scabs dotting the crook of his arm, laughed, and rested a palm on the back of my neck.

Jimmy said he had died, technically, because his heart stopped for six minutes, but someone with Narcan resurrected him. He nodded his head toward the bartender. "They keep that shit in stock here."

"You're telling me you died here and still come?"

"Only place I drink. These people here are my guardian angels."

"But nothing that happened made you change?"

He studied my face for a moment. I watched his for some sign of, I don't know, fear or regret, but he showed neither. "Change?"

I put back the dregs of my beer. "You know, you almost killed yourself." I didn't know how to put words to it. "You got real close to death. You stepped on the cliff's edge and slipped off and came back. But you're saying you're still using the shit, right? You don't worry you're gonna die?"

Another shot of whiskey appeared on the bar top in front of Jimmy. He sunk it with a flick of his head, then considered what I was asking him. "Truth is, I thought about dying all the time, even before. Shit, that was half of what we talked about at prayer group, you remember? I just got used to it, I guess. I don't want it to happen, but it don't bother me none knowing it will."

I asked if he had a number I could reach him at, but he said he traded his phone for a bag and never had enough scratch to replace it. He put back another shot, then took hold of my shoulder. "You got work?"

"Nothing worth a shit. Mowing lawns. Planting bushes in yards. Weed whacking. Whatever I can find."

"But you're getting paid?"

"Little bit. Not enough."

He raised a finger, then pointed it at the empty shot glass in front of him. The bartender came over and refilled it. "It's on my friend here," Jimmy said. He slapped me on the back, slammed back the shot glass, and walked out of the bar. The bartender turned up the music. A group of men at a table behind me shouted at one another. On the muted TV in the corner, the nightly news showed a clip of bulldozers outside the Han Gil. The camera zoomed out, panned across the ruins of gnarled steel and shattered concrete. The news ended and cut to the ballgame. The Rangers were down by two in the last inning. I killed my beer and looked at the dim lights above the liquor shelf, stared at their dull pulse for so long it felt as if my eyes might burn away from the inside out.

ACKNOWLEDGMENTS

With many thanks to the editors of the literary magazines that published versions of the stories included in this collection: *Five South*, *Pithead Chapel*, *The Coachella Review*, *Porter House Review*, *Cowboy Jamboree*, *South 85 Journal*, *Epiphany: A Literary Journal*, *Cleaver*, *Peatsmoke Journal*, *New World Writing Quarterly*, *The Broadkill Review*, *The Barcelona Review*, and *Flash Fiction Magazine*. Special thanks to *Porter House Review* for nominating "General Holy War" for a Pushcart Prize, and a lot of gratitude to *Pithead Chapel* for awarding "Rent Money" third place in the 2021 Larry Brown Short Fiction Prize. Thank you to The de Groot Foundation for picking me as a 2024 Writer of Note and supporting the work that went into *A History of Heartache*.

For their feedback on earlier versions of these stories, I'm grateful to my mentors, teachers, and classmates at the University of Nebraska–Omaha's MFA program: Patricia Lear, Kate Gale, Jim Peterson, Kevin Clouther, and Marya Hornbacher, among others. A special thanks to Alan Heathcock for his guidance, feedback, and insistence that I push several of these stories into darker, more complicated places. Endless thanks go to M.A. Boswell, my friend and writing comrade. For her encouragement and support, I'm beyond indebted to Jenny. For their boundless patience and support, I'm thankful to my family and friends, especially my mother, my stepfather, and my brother.

PATRICK STRICKLAND is a writer and journalist from Texas. He is the author of three nonfiction books on the far right and migration: *You Can Kill Each Other After I Leave* (2025), *The Marauders* (2022), and *Alerta! Alerta! Snapshots of Europe's Antifascist Struggle* (2018). His reporting has appeared in *The New York Review of Books*, *The Guardian*, *Time*, *Al Jazeera*, and elsewhere. His fiction has appeared in *Epiphany*, *Pithead Chapel*, and the *Porter House Review*, among others. In 2024, The de Groot Foundation picked him as a writer of note. He is currently the managing editor of Inkstick Media.